*Ecstasy Romance*®

## "IS SOMETHING WRONG?" CHRISTOPHER ASKED.

"You mean something *other* than the fact that you're getting ready to steal one of my station's top accounts?" Adrienne inquired bluntly.

His face lightened in a smile. "Oh, I see. Don't worry. Stan Halloway is extremely loyal to KXMZ. He's not interested in advertising with us."

"Then you've already asked him?"

"Of course I have. You can't blame a man for trying. You would have done the same thing if you were in my position."

She probably would have, Adrienne acknowledged inwardly. "You can get me that drink now."

"What's your pleasure?"

Perhaps because she felt so relieved about the Halloway account, she answered with a coyness that surprised even her. "I don't think we should get into that. Why don't we just stick to drinks for the moment?"

His chuckle was low and appreciative. "I'm willing to accommodate in any way I can."

## CANDLELIGHT ECSTASY ROMANCES®

# NOT TOO PERFECT

*Candice Adams*

*A CANDLELIGHT ECSTASY ROMANCE*®

Published by
Dell Publishing Co., Inc.
1 Dag Hammarskjold Plaza
New York, New York 10017

Dell ® TM 681510, Dell Publishing Co., Inc.

Candlelight Ecstasy Romance®, 1,203,540, is a registered
trademark of Dell Publishing Co., Inc., New York, New York.

ISBN: 0-440-16451-6

Printed in the United States of America
First printing—January 1985

*For Sandra*

To Our Readers:

We have been delighted with your enthusiastic response to Candlelight Ecstasy Romances®, and we thank you for the interest you have shown in this exciting series.

In the upcoming months we will continue to present the distinctive, sensuous love stories you have come to expect only from Ecstasy. We look forward to bringing you many more books from your favorite authors and also the very finest work from new authors of contemporary romantic fiction.

As always, we are striving to present the unique, absorbing love stories that you enjoy most—books that are more than ordinary romance.

Your suggestions and comments are always welcome. Please write to us at the address below.

Sincerely,

The Editors
Candlelight Romances
1 Dag Hammarskjold Plaza
New York, New York 10017

# CHAPTER ONE

The bars along St. Louis's Laclede's Landing had begun to flourish once again, frequented by a crowd of trendy young sophisticates. The old buildings accepted that fact as placidly as they had once accepted the wild young men on their way west in search of gold, the ax-wielding Carry Nation, and the unkempt hoboes who had slept in their doorways until the recent renovations. As the Mississippi River lapped nearby, it listened impassively to the music and laughter floating out of the open doors.

Inside a cozy bar Adrienne Donnelly sat with two male co-workers and watched the waitress set drinks on their table. She felt lethargically content as she sipped at her white wine and tapped her foot in time to the music from a small combo in the corner. She liked the comfortable atmosphere of the bar with its antique pine tables and chairs, brass footrail, and Art Deco mirrors. Through the plate glass front window she could see old buildings with cast-iron fronts standing like sentinels from the past.

"We've had a good response to that question-answer

series, haven't we, Adrienne?" Mark, the blond-haired man beside her, asked.

She nodded agreeably, still tapping her foot to the music.

"Are you thinking of expanding it into an hour show?"

Adrienne pushed back the copper-colored wisps of hair that drifted across her forehead and considered his question thoughtfully. "I don't know yet. I'll have to see if the listeners continue to follow the show." She'd learned early in her radio career that what the audience liked in moderation, it didn't necessarily love in quantity. One of her first mistakes as a station manager had been to expand into a two-hour show a program the listeners had enjoyed only for an hour.

She glanced up as a napkin floated to the floor near her feet. Absently she picked it up and put it on the table by her drink, then joined in the laughter at one of Mark's jokes. Mark was the sales manager, and her other companion, Gregg, a trim man with a receding hairline, was program director at KXMZ, the radio station at which she was general manager.

Another napkin fluttered past her legs, creating a mild breeze as it wafted by her navy linen skirt, then settled on the floor beside her high, slim heels. This time, before she bent to pick it up, she glanced over at the man, sitting in a booth by himself, who was so carelessly losing napkin after napkin. He was a handsome dark-haired man who smiled genially at her. She smiled distantly in acknowledgment and laid the second napkin over the first.

"Hey, there's something written on that. What does it

10

say?" Gregg leaned across Adrienne and peered at the words scrawled on the cocktail napkin. "It says, 'Read the first napkin.' Okay." He picked up the other one and read aloud, " 'I've done a careful survey and have decided you have the nicest legs in the place.' " Gregg lifted his head and grinned cheekily toward the lone man. "Thanks," he called, touching his hair with exaggerated daintiness.

"I think he means me," Mark said objectively.

Adrienne couldn't repress a smile as she shook her head and sighed. "I don't believe this."

Mark gave her a consoling pat on the back. "You certainly don't think he meant *you,* do you? Why would he notice a skinny redhead when he has two gorgeous men to pick from?" Mark motioned for the napkin's author to come over.

The stranger stood up and sauntered toward them. He was tall, Adrienne noted, but he moved with the litheness of a well-conditioned athlete. Up close she could see that he was very handsome. She judged him to be around thirty. Beneath casually brushed coal black hair his features were classically sculpted. His eyes were blue-gray, and they glimmered with amusement, although his mouth was perfectly straight.

Mark extended his hand. "Hi, I'm Mark Wiley, and this is Gregg. Oh, and Adrienne," he added offhandedly. "Gregg and I are having a little problem deciding which of us you thought had such great legs."

The dark-haired stranger grinned. "I can see where that would be a problem."

11

Being in radio, Adrienne noticed people's voices, and this man had a husky, velvet voice that would have made detergent commercials sound like exercises in erotica. But his voice wasn't his only asset. His mouth was soft and sensual, particularly now as it filled with laughter. And if his blue-gray eyes were the window to his soul, he had a beguiling, mysterious one.

"From where I was sitting, you all looked terrific." His eyes skimmed the table and came finally to rest on Adrienne. "Actually, however, I thought the lady's were especially attractive. I'm afraid I have more of a weakness for women's legs than men's," he explained apologetically.

She smiled at him from beneath the fringe of her lashes and basked in the glow of his compliment. At twenty-seven she knew, or should have known, not to put too much emphasis on compliments given by strange men in bars. But when he added that irresistible smile, she admitted to feeling something fluttery that harked back to her teen years.

There were groans from Adrienne's two companions. "Just when I thought I was going to get someone to pay for my drink," Gregg grumbled.

"Why don't you join us?" Mark suggested. "You can at least pay for Adrienne's drinks. If you can afford it," he cautioned, moving over to make room. "She usually drinks herself under the table, and we have to carry her out."

The newcomer slid into the empty seat beside Adrienne. "I'll take my chances."

The stranger's merriment transmitted itself to her, and

she lowered her voice and confided to him, "You can't believe a word they say. These men are trusties from Leavenworth, and I'm their warden. Watch your wallet."

"I will."

The lightness of their banter did not keep Adrienne from noticing that the stranger's eyes were combing her face in warm appraisal. Ned hadn't looked at her with such obvious approval in some time. But then, she reminded herself staunchly, Ned had lots of other good qualities.

The stranger motioned the waitress over and ordered a fresh drink. "By the way, I'm Christopher Ames."

"Christopher Ames," Gregg repeated, furrowing his brow in thought. "That name sounds kind of familiar."

Adrienne nodded. In fact she thought she'd heard it within the past week or so. But she was sure she'd never met him; if she had, she definitely would have remembered. Even a woman who was involved with another man couldn't overlook the way amusement further enriched the sexiness of Christopher Ames's voice or the way the lights lost themselves in the blackness of his hair. Even the way he brushed his index finger across the high bridge of his nose had a subtle allure.

"I'm the new president and general manager of KTOO," Christopher supplied helpfully.

"Ah." Adrienne exchanged covert glances with her coworkers before busying herself pushing back the red-gold strands of hair that had slipped forward onto her forehead from her casual arrangement of soft waves. The radio station he had mentioned, KTOO, was so far down

13

in the ratings it would have to reach up to touch bottom. On the other hand, *her* radio station, KXMZ, rode the crest of the ratings chart and had the largest share of the young to middle-age adult audience.

"Well, uh, that's interesting, Christopher," Mark said tactfully. "Very interesting." He swiftly changed the subject. "How about another drink? I'll buy."

"Thanks, but my glass is still full," Christopher said amiably. "What sort of business are you people in?"

"We're in, ah, radio, too." Gregg occupied himself straightening the cuffs of his shirt.

"You are! Well, great. I hope it doesn't make any difference that I'm the competition." Christopher glanced around with one dark eyebrow lifted in question.

"Oh, no, none at all," three people hastened to assure him.

Adrienne knew Mark and Gregg both were thinking what she was: that poor little KTOO wasn't any competition. It simply limped along, supplying a few old diehard fans with last week's news and some moldy records.

"Good," Christopher said pleasantly. "Well, since I'm new to St. Louis, maybe you can tell me some good places to eat."

She was relieved to have the subject directed away from radio. While Mark began to list the merits of an Italian restaurant, Gregg waxed eloquent on an out-of-the-way Armenian place. Soon the two men had forgotten that Christopher had asked a question and were busy discussing restaurants between themselves.

But Adrienne's attention was more fully occupied with

14

Christopher Ames. He might be with a station that was a loser, but he definitely had a great deal going for him personally. He was one of the most undeniably handsome men she'd ever met, and she couldn't keep from looking at him.

Their eyes met, and she smiled pleasantly. "Where did you work before coming here, Christopher?"

"Miami."

"What station were you with there?"

"I wasn't with a radio station at the time," he told her. "I was in market research."

Her eyes clouded in confusion. "But you've been associated with radio before now, haven't you?"

"No, I haven't," he said blandly. "I'm new to the business."

"I see." Adrienne dived into her drink to cover her astonishment. Only a station like KTOO would hire a manager who didn't know the first thing about the business. Suddenly she felt sorry for the man sitting beside her. Although he seemed self-confident, he obviously had no idea what he was getting into. Being a station manager wasn't something a person could step into cold and expect to succeed at.

He trailed his fingers through his thick black hair, creating a tiny row of furrows. "What sort of work do you do at your station?"

"I'm the manager."

A grin spread over his face, and he lifted his glass to her. "Here's to station managers. May we both have success."

She raised her glass wordlessly. No, the poor man had no idea what he was wading into. For the moment, however, she let that fact slide to the back of her mind. Whatever shortcomings Christopher Ames might have in the field of communications, he certainly didn't lack anything in the way of looks and polish. He appeared very Ivy League in a dark gray suit, a crisp white shirt, and an oxblood tie. His hands were tanned and manicured, and his smile had the power to warm and put its recipient at ease.

"How long have you been in town?" she asked conversationally, at the same time throwing a surreptitious glance at the Art Deco mirror behind Christopher and trying to measure herself as he must be seeing her. Because her face was partially shadowed in the bar's uneven light, the hollows beneath her high cheekbones were exaggerated, and her brown eyes looked wider and darker than usual. Her hair was too fine and silky to conform rigidly to a hairstyle, so she had to satisfy herself with the loose, carefree waves that just touched her collar. Although she brushed her hair back away from her face, a few tendrils had slid forward and now curled around her forehead.

"I just got into town this week," Christopher said. "I'm still in a hotel, but I think I've found an apartment to move into." He nodded toward her empty glass. "Care for something else to drink?"

Adrienne shook her head. "No, thanks." She got giggly and a little klutzy when she drank too much, and she didn't want Christopher to see her like that. She wanted him to like her but not *too* much. She'd learned a long time ago that men like him meant trouble for her. He was so self-assured, so excitingly masculine, and his smile was so charming it almost persuaded her to trust him. But he was too much like another man she'd known. . . . Besides, she and Ned had been dating for several months.

Mark leaned over to announce that he was leaving. "I'd like to stay, but Sarah's waiting for me. You know how wives are," he added with a sigh of mock exasperation.

"I'm afraid I don't," Christopher said.

Adrienne was aware that his eyes once again lingered on her. She realized how easy it would be to let those smoky blue eyes hypnotize her into forgetting that she was a sensible, realistic woman. She'd better leave before that happened, she told herself and pushed back her chair. "I've got to get home, too. Bye, Gregg." She turned to Christopher with a polite smile. "It was nice meeting you."

His eyes ran over her as she stood up. "I'm glad we met. I hope I'll see you again."

The tone of his voice conveyed his interest in her, but she kept her tone purposely nonchalant as she replied, "Oh, I'm sure we'll run into each other somewhere or other. The radio stations here in town are often involved in the same community affairs." She threw a farewell smile around the table. "Bye, everyone." But the image she carried with her as she walked out the open doors of the bar was that of Christopher propping his chin on the back of his knuckles and watching her speculatively. It had been a decidedly sexy gesture, and the sooner she forgot it, the better. Christopher definitely wasn't her type.

"I'll walk you to your car," Mark volunteered as they stepped outside.

"Thanks." The September evenings brought darkness to the city earlier and earlier, and she was glad of Mark's company as they strode by old buildings that had been built after the Civil War and had recently been renovated into fashionable bars and restaurants.

"Christopher seems like a nice guy," Mark observed idly. Their footsteps echoed on the brick sidewalk.

"Mmmm."

"I wonder if he knows yet that KTOO is a real dog. I guess he'll find out soon enough." Mark chuckled. "The awards ceremony is next week, and the only prize his station is likely to win is the door prize."

"KTOO has a very good weekly program for the elderly," Adrienne said, trying to be fair.

Mark laughed heartily as they stopped beside her small blue car. "Oh, yes, I forgot about that enlightening program. But you do have to admit he's got his work cut out for him if he's going to bring in any new listeners. Practically everyone in the city who listens to middle-of-the-road stations tunes in to us."

She tapped him on the arm in mild reproof. "I know, but I'm trying not to be smug about that."

"Aw, go ahead and be smug." Mark exhorted her cheerfully. "You deserve it. You work hard to keep our programming good."

She smiled. "Thanks for the compliment. And good night." For just a moment before she started the car she allowed herself to reread the napkins she had carried from the bar with her. Then she started the car and put Christopher Ames firmly out of her mind.

The awards banquet was a posh affair at an elegant downtown hotel. Adrienne wore a red strapless gown with a tiny ruffle above her bust and a bodice which fitted tightly to the waist, below which folds of silk swirled to the floor. She had pinned a tiny cluster of baby's breath above one ear.

The burgundy carpet was so thick in the lobby her tall heels disappeared into it, and she had to grab Ned's arm for support. He looked at her absently, then linked his arm more firmly in hers. "You shouldn't have worn those shoes," he told her matter-of-factly. "You should have worn something comfortable."

"You're right," she agreed, stifling an impish impulse to tell him her tennis shoes were dirty. Ned generally had a good sense of humor, but it was seldom in evidence on occasions when he was trussed up in a stiff collar and a cummerbund. Ned hated dressing up. "Why a tuxedo?" he had demanded when she had told him about the banquet. He'd still been wondering that aloud in the car on the way over.

"How long will this thing last?" he asked as they stepped into the ballroom.

Adrienne shrugged vaguely. "I'm not sure." It seemed the better part of valor not to tell him they probably wouldn't leave before one or two in the morning. She nodded toward the corner. "There's the bar. Why don't you go teach them how you like your Scotch and soda?"

As he went off in one direction, Mark and his wife, Sarah, approached from another, and Adrienne stopped to talk with them.

"Love your dress, Adrienne."

"Thanks, Sarah. Yours is pretty, too."

"Looks as if they're going to have a big crowd," Mark observed. The trio made small talk until Ned returned with a drink for himself and Perrier water for Adrienne. " 'lo, Ned. How's the world been treating you?" Mark asked.

"Can't complain."

As the two men exchanged laconic conversation, Adrienne sipped at her Perrier and glanced around. Several long tables had been set up at one side of the large room, with a speaker's table facing the other tables. The remaining half of the room had been left open for the dancing that would ensue after the awards ceremony. Ned wasn't crazy about dancing either.

Adrienne turned back to her companions and found the men engrossed in a conversation about the Cardinals' last season. She and Sarah drifted over to chat with another group of people.

Twenty minutes later Adrienne was laughing at a description of a disc jockey's first work experience when someone came up beside her.

"Hello, there."

Looking up, she smiled at the tall man who had joined

them. She hadn't consciously known that she had been looking forward to seeing Christopher Ames, but now that he was here, she felt a surge of exhilaration, and her smile widened. "Why, hello, Mr. Ames. Do you know my friends?" She lifted her glass and indicated the circle of half a dozen people.

He gave them the benefit of his pulse-quickening smile. "No, I don't."

Adrienne made the introductions. While murmurs of greeting were exchanged, she touched the baby's breath in her hair and studied Christopher through the veil of her lashes. He looked tall and dignified in his black tuxedo with satin lapels, starched white shirt, and black bow tie. And he mingled easily, she realized as he fell into a discussion with a man standing nearby. Given a good radio station to manage, he just might have been able to make a go of it in spite of his lack of experience. But of course, he was stuck with KTOO—and enough said on that subject.

"There you are," Ned said as he stopped beside her.

Adrienne glanced up at her date, then back at Christopher. It was impossible not to compare the two men. Ned was also tall, but he had brown hair where Christopher's was midnight black. Ned's features were regular, but they weren't etched in smoothly perfect planes the way Christopher's were. And Christopher had a quality that would lure any woman; it was a strange mixture of dynamic masculinity and the charm of a mischievous little boy. Guiltily Adrienne brought an end to the comparison. She wouldn't have wanted Ned to compare her to a startlingly beautiful woman.

Someone tapped on the microphone, and when the chatter of voices subsided, the announcement that dinner would be served shortly was made. "Please find your places, everyone." A general scramble followed as people looked for their name cards on the four long tables. When Adrienne finally located her chair, she found Christopher already seated next to her.

"Hi." He was sitting with his arms folded across his chest smiling up at her.

She arched her eyebrows in surprise. "My, what a coincidence," she murmured.

"No coincidence. I was near the back, but I moved up here so I could hear the speaker better. Besides, I wanted to sit near you."

Again Adrienne realized how easily she could become entranced with those blue-gray eyes. But she wasn't going to. Neither was she going to flirt with this man, even though he obviously was flirting with her. Clearly he didn't realize she was with Ned. "Have you met my date?" she asked, looping her arm through Ned's. "This is Ned Riley. Ned, this is Christopher Ames, the new president and general manager of KTOO."

"Glad to meet you." Christopher stood and shook hands, then looked around the room. "My own date is here somewhere."

Adrienne looked around, too. She wanted to see the kind of woman a man like Christopher dated. It was simple curiosity, that was all.

"Never mind. I'm sure my date won't have any trouble finding me," Christopher said as he sat down again. Adrienne was seated between him and Ned, and Christopher leaned past her to ask, "What line of work are you in, Ned?"

"I have my own printing business."

"Great!" Christopher said enthusiastically. "Where are you located? Maybe our station can use you."

Adrienne knew it was the first time all evening anyone had displayed even a hint of interest in Ned's business. Beaming, Ned whipped out a business card, and the two men began to discuss offset printing like old friends. She was pleased to see that Ned was enjoying himself for the first time that evening. And she had wanted Christopher to realize she was not available. Yet perversely, now that Christopher was paying her no attention, she couldn't help feeling a little disappointed.

A dumpy man with a cigar protruding from his mouth slid into the seat beside Christopher, who grinned at him. "Ah, here's my date now. Adrienne, you probably know Walt Taylor. He's the owner of KTOO. Walt Taylor, I'd like you to meet Ned Riley. Ned owns a printing shop, and I'm very impressed with what he's been telling me about his color machine."

Walt nodded his interest as he worked on lighting his cigar. "Really?"

The three men began to talk about printing. Adrienne was glad when the program began. A guest speaker talked at some length about the great tradition of radio. They all listened politely, but Adrienne knew they were really here for the awards, and the animation showed in their faces when the awards ceremony finally began. KXMZ won a number of accolades, as did several other stations. But the one conspicuous by the few times it was mentioned was KTOO. At first Adrienne felt uncomfortable sitting next to KTOO's new manager, but Christopher seemed unperturbed by the fact that his station was winning few prizes. He applauded enthusiastically as every prize was announced and bent forward to congratulate her each time KXMZ won something.

"That was terrific," he said when all the awards had been named and people had begun to chat again. "Of course, I'm new in town, but I'm sure all the winners were very deserving. Congratulations, Adrienne. Your station did very well."

"Thank you," she said self-consciously. She could scarcely say anything about *his* station, so she busied herself tucking back a wisp of her hair.

A few moments later the band began to play, and people drifted toward the dance floor. Although Adrienne cast a longing glance in that direction, Ned merely sipped at his drink and appeared not to notice.

But Christopher did. She saw his eyes go from her to Ned with a faintly quizzical expression. "Do you mind if I steal a dance with your date, Ned?" Christopher asked and nodded toward Walt with a wry smile. "My own date has two left feet."

"Yeah, we're terrible together," Walt agreed and reached for another cigar.

"Fine with me," Ned said equably.

Christopher turned to her and lifted the wing of one dark eyebrow. "Adrienne?"

She nodded. "I'd love to." In fact, she'd been hoping to dance with him sometime in the course of the evening.

He rose and pulled back her chair. A moment later his arm firmly encircled her waist, and they were moving together in time to the beguiling music of a slow dance. She could smell the musk scent of his aftershave, feel the light pressure of his body against hers, and hear the rustle of her silk gown as they moved through a turn together. And all the while the musicians played a beautifully sad melody. The mood was, quite frankly, romantic.

But that was not what she should be feeling, Adrienne chided herself. This man was not her date. Neither was he the type that would be good for her, in spite of the strong feelings he was provoking in her. Bobby had also had the power to catch her up in the spell of his ebullient smile. In fact, she'd been so entranced by him that she'd been blinded to his faults. But she had been younger then and less experienced. Now she knew enough to be wary of the kind of man who made her heart race too fast. Yet her head was almost touching his shoulder, and she felt curiously content in his arms. Surely it couldn't hurt to let herself enjoy the feeling for a few moments longer, she reasoned.

Just then another couple danced by. "Hey, Adrienne," the man called. "Congratulations! Your station really cleaned up tonight."

"Thanks," she murmured and stole a glance up at Christopher to measure his reaction. He was smiling genially. Disturbed by the absence of any trace of jealousy or resentment, she asked bluntly, "Doesn't it bother you that KTOO didn't win anything?"

He blinked. "That isn't true. We won the award for the best five-minute crime prevention special on a Wednesday afternoon."

Adrienne couldn't be sure if his blue eyes were twinkling or if it was merely the reflection from the chandeliers. But even if he wasn't actually taking his station's failure in good humor, he certainly didn't seem to be taking it seriously. And that dismayed her. She had always cared a lot about her work and been competitive. It was a quality she felt was necessary to get ahead in the business world, and she had definitely needed it to keep KXMZ at the top of the ratings chart. Yet Christopher seemed content to manage a losing station.

His arm tightened around her as he drew her into another turn. "Let's not talk business right now. Let's just enjoy the music, okay?"

Adrienne nodded. She was perfectly willing to do that. But she couldn't help thinking what a shame it was that this handsome, charming man lacked what it took to put KTOO on the fast track. Then he dipped his head closer to hers, and his breath tickled at her neck, producing such a delicious sensation that she forgot everything else.

## CHAPTER TWO

Christopher had just returned home from work and was entering his bedroom to change into his tux when the doorbell rang. He opened the front door and looked down at two small girls.

"We're selling Girl Scout cookies," one of them lisped.

He smiled. "You are?"

They both nodded mutely.

"And you would like me to buy some?" he suggested helpfully.

Again they nodded.

They drove a hard bargain, Christopher considered in amusement as he pulled out his billfold. "I'll take two boxes from each of you." After helping them figure out what his bill came to, he paid, bought an extra box for the children to share, and started back into the bedroom.

Too bad it wasn't as easy for a radio station to sell advertising time as it was for angelic-looking little girls to sell cookies. He'd have it made if it were. But then, he decided as he shrugged out of his soft wool suit jacket, he wouldn't have taken this job if it hadn't offered him a challenge.

And his new job was definitely going to be a challenge. He could see that KTOO needed a housecleaning from top to bottom. During the week he had been at the station he'd already drawn up an eight-page list of improvements to be made that ranged from redecorating the reception area to completely changing the program format.

He opened one of the boxes and munched on a chocolate mint cookie while he adjusted his pleated tuxedo shirt. Then he stepped back and surveyed himself in the full-length mirror on the bedroom door. "You look like a headwaiter," he told his reflection as he reached for another cookie. Ah, well, it was all for the cause. If he was going to drag KTOO out of the basement, he was going to have to circulate among people who owned companies and bought advertising time.

Sitting through the awards ceremony last Friday night had also been for the cause, although he had enjoyed some very pleasant moments dancing with Adrienne Donnelly. He liked her. She was an attractive woman. Not beautiful, but . . . scintillating with her saucy smile, graceful movements, and mink brown eyes. He could still recall the April smell of her hair. He would like to have gotten to know her better, but there had been one major drawback: She had been with another man.

Christopher sat on the edge of the bed, picked up a soft cloth, and began rubbing a high gloss onto his black leather shoes. What in the devil was Adrienne doing dating Ned Riley? While he found Ned likable enough, the man was grave and quiet and clearly lacked Adrienne's playful spirit and sparkle. And Christopher had noticed there had been no warm touches or gentle looks exchanged between them. Adrienne and Ned had seemed to be good friends and nothing more.

After making a final pass at his shoes, Christopher laid the cloth aside, smiling reflectively as he recalled Adrienne's question: "Doesn't it bother you that KTOO didn't win anything?" She obviously mistook his acceptance for resignation. She couldn't be more wrong. With each award that had gone to another station, he had silently strengthened his resolve to make KTOO next year's winner.

And if there was one thing he was good at, it was turning things around. He had learned as much the hard way, starting with himself when he had been on a downhill slide to nowhere.

Adrienne was putting a final dab of green facial mask on her cheek when the doorbell rang.

"Rats." Tying her white terry-cloth robe more securely around herself, she crossed the bare oak floor into the living room and called through the closed door, "Who is it?"

"Kelly."

Kelly, who lived in the condominium next door, had been a friend since college. Adrienne slipped off the dead bolt, opened the door just enough for Kelly to squeeze through, then closed it again.

The lithe brunette folded her arms across her chest and

29

looked Adrienne over critically. "I think you got carried away with the green eye shadow," she decided.

Adrienne tossed her head regally. "You may make fun of the way I look now, but wait until you see the results. I'm going to look 'radiant, glowing, and exciting.' That's what the instructions on the bottle promised." She motioned Kelly to a chair in the living room.

It was a comfortable room with a sliding glass door that led out onto a balcony. The late-afternoon sun shafted in through the glass, highlighting the beige sofa and fuzzy white area rug covering the bare floor.

Kelly made herself at home in a wicker rocker and tucked her feet under her. Casually she picked up the newspaper and began flipping through it. "What time are you going out tonight?"

"We're not. Ned's working late."

The other woman lifted her eyebrows in surprise. "I thought you *always* went out on Tuesdays. Don't tell me you and Ned are going to stop being creatures of habit?"

Adrienne tried to wrinkle her nose but was prevented from doing so by the dried mask. She settled for tossing her head again. "What's wrong with being creatures of habit? I'm perfectly happy in my relationship with Ned." They were comfortable with each other, and neither made demands on the other.

"You're happy for now," Kelly said as she turned a page of the paper. "But you know it won't last. It never does. You just can't make a commitment to a man."

Adrienne sat on the couch and began placidly applying a coat of clear nail polish to her fingernails. "I don't know why you're always saying that. Of course, I can commit myself to a man. Why, I've been dating Ned for months, and before that Jeffrey and I were very serious about each other."

The sound that emerged from behind the paper was a cross between a grunt and a sniff. "Before Jeffrey it was Arthur." Lowering the paper, Kelly focused clear green eyes on Adrienne. "And I don't remember who it was before that. Ever since Bobby died, you've followed this pattern of picking someone you know isn't right for you. Ned's so damned colorless. Don't get me wrong, he's nice, but he doesn't have any glitter. He's safe and secure, but he doesn't excite you." Heedless of the fact that she was crumpling the paper, she leaned forward fervently. "But you're interested in a man only as long as you know you aren't in any danger of being carried away by your feelings."

"You've been reading too many pop psychology books." Adrienne continued impassively stroking polish over her nails. It wasn't the first time Kelly had brought up this theory, but she was wrong. Adrienne wasn't afraid of letting go of her feelings, but she wasn't going to do it with the wrong man. As for consciously selecting a man who had a flaw, *all* men had flaws. If she waited around for the perfect man, she'd spend precious little time dating.

"You've forgotten what it's like to be really affected by a man," Kelly said as she ran her fingers through her long brown hair. "When was the last time you felt breathless with a man?"

31

Adrienne smothered a chuckle. "When Jeffrey and I used to go jogging."

Kelly shot her a dark look. "All right, I can see you don't want to talk about men." She turned back to the paper.

As it happened, however, Adrienne did want to talk about men or at least one particular man. She put the nail polish aside and glanced idly toward the television, all the while blowing on her nails to dry them. "Did I tell you about the man I met at the bar last week?"

"I don't think so."

"His name is Christopher Ames. Anyway, he was at the awards ceremony. We danced together a few times." Three times, to be exact, Adrienne recalled as she looked pensively into space. Christopher had also kissed her at the end of the evening. It had been a very proper kiss— on the cheek—which had left her wondering what a real kiss from Christopher would feel like. Any mouth that could turn upward into such a seductive smile could surely impart delicious kisses that would eddy over her mouth like . . .

Kelly nudged her with her foot. "Go on, what were you saying about this guy?"

Adrienne corralled her wandering thoughts and shrugged. "Oh—just that I saw him again. He seems very nice," she concluded casually. She wasn't sure why she had brought Christopher's name into the conversation, except that she had wanted to talk about him. She had since the night of the banquet.

Kelly studied her curiously. "Are you interested in him?"

"Yes—that is, I mean, no." Adrienne began fluffing briskly at her hair. "He's too easygoing and carefree for my taste." She preferred more steady, dependable men.

"But you like him?" Kelly pressed.

"He's okay," Adrienne said with deliberate indifference. Instead of thinking of his assets, like his lean masculine body, she forced herself to concentrate on his shortcomings. "I'm not sure how well he's going to do managing a radio station. He's nice, but he doesn't seem to have the drive and competitive edge a person needs to get ahead in this business."

"Why do you say that?" Kelly asked.

"Oh, just from the impression I got at the banquet. He didn't act very concerned that his station won only one award."

"Doesn't sound as if he'll go far," Kelly agreed and disappeared behind the newspaper again.

"No," Adrienne murmured and didn't know why that fact made her feel vaguely restless and disturbed. What difference did it make to her if Christopher was a success or not? He was still practically a stranger. After all, she'd seen him only twice.

"I'll get us something to drink." She rose abruptly, then busied herself in the kitchen before returning to the living room a few moments later with a soft drink for each of them.

Kelly accepted hers without looking up. "What did you say that guy's name was?"

"Christopher Ames." Adrienne sat down on the sofa again.

"There's a picture of him in the paper. And a story."

Adrienne leaned forward, her interest quickening. "What does it say?"

"That he's from Houston and that his first job was selling popcorn at a movie theater." Kelly looked over the top of the paper and smirked. "I'd buy anything he was selling. He's a hunk."

She couldn't argue with that. "What else does it say?"

"Um, that he was in charge of a research firm in Miami until recently. It ends with a quote from him saying that KTOO is a station on the move."

Adrienne relaxed back in the sofa and giggled. "Does he say if it's moving up or down?" Immediately she was contrite. "I shouldn't make fun of poor KTOO. I'm sure Christopher had no idea when he took the job what an underdog the station was. And he doesn't even have any radio experience," she lamented before taking a sip of cola. The next time she saw him she might tactfully let him know she was willing to answer any questions he had about the business.

"Want to see his picture?" Kelly asked.

At Adrienne's nod Kelly folded back the page and held it up. The grainy black-and-white photo didn't do justice to Christopher's mirthful eyes, well-cut features, and lush ebony hair. And there was no way it could convey that indefinable aura of masculine charisma that enveloped him.

"He's better-looking in person," Adrienne said.

"How can he be?" Kelly sighed wistfully. "He's perfect."

Adrienne gazed solemnly at the picture. No, Christopher wasn't perfect. At least not for her. He was too handsome and too charming for her. Worse, he seemed to evoke in her the same reckless feelings Bobby had. And she surely didn't want to feel that way again.

The sidelight of the radio business that Adrienne enjoyed most was community service work. Last year she'd been on the Council for the Blind, and the year before she'd been on a committee to raise money for a center for retarded people. But the volunteer work she was doing now was by far the most challenging and possibly the most rewarding she'd ever done. She was cochairman of the fund drive for the Hopewell Home for Boys. Frank Boswell, the president of the classical music station, was cochairing the drive with her.

From the moment she'd accepted the position two months ago she'd wanted to do more than attend committee meetings and listen to recommendations from a board. That was too impersonal. "I want to get to know the boys myself and find out what their lives are like and what I personally can do to make them better," she had explained to Boswell at the time.

Boswell, a thin man with a drooping mustache, had listened to her doubtfully.

"Of course, whatever you want to do is up to you," Adrienne added. "I don't want to push you into anything."

35

"I suppose it couldn't hurt to get to know the boys," he had conceded.

Looking at Boswell now, however, Adrienne thought he was regretting his decision. It was a beautiful fall Saturday afternoon, and they were standing in the outfield behind the austere brick buildings of the boys' home. Adrienne's baseball cap was pulled down low on her forehead, and she held her mitt at the ready. Kenny was up at bat, and he always drove the ball straight at Boswell, who at the moment looked unhappy and apprehensive.

"I don't understand why that kid always aims at me," he complained.

Adrienne heard the crack of the ball against the bat, and then the ball torpedoed straight for Boswell. She ran to catch it while Boswell fled from it.

"Got it!" she cried as her mitt closed securely around the baseball.

Kenny surrendered third base and clumped morosely back to home plate.

Boswell returned to his position and carefully straightened his shirt. "Will he be up at bat again?"

She couldn't help smiling. "No, this game is almost over."

"Thank heavens!"

At that she laughed aloud. Granted, the ball games were an ordeal for Boswell, but she thought both she and he were developing more insight into the boys, and that might help them think up ways to raise money.

Adrienne knew from reading the statistics that the boys who lived at the home ranged in age from nine to sixteen. Some of them had been abandoned by their parents or had been placed there by welfare workers because of abuse or neglect. Some of the boys had even come voluntarily.

But what the reports hadn't told her was what the kids were like. Some of them, she had come to realize, were content here, while others yearned constantly to return to their homes but couldn't because of alcoholic or irresponsible parents. She'd begun to know the boys by name and had discovered among them all types of personalities. Some were open, affectionate kids who throve on hugs and words of praise. Some were little con men who would try to borrow money they had no intention of repaying. And there were a few boys who were sullen and opened up to no one. Malcolm was one of those, and he had become Adrienne's special project, although she couldn't truthfully say she'd accomplished much with him so far.

The baseball game ended, and the winning team scrambled off the field, shouting exultantly. The losers, Adrienne's team, trooped off, mumbling among themselves.

Boswell came up beside her as they walked toward the building. "Last year I worked on a committee to preserve the elm trees," he said wistfully. "It was very peaceful, and no one aimed fast balls at me."

"You'll do a lot more good this year," she said consolingly before she stopped to push eleven-year-old Danny's cap playfully down over his eyes. "I've got a couple of ideas for fund raising. When can we get together to discuss them?" She was anxious to start work to raise money. Since Hopewell Home operated without government assistance, money shortages were always a problem. The building needed constant repairs, and the home was understaffed for the forty boys who currently lived there.

"I'm not sure of my schedule," Boswell said. "Maybe next week. I'll call you."

She nodded.

They parted outside the door of the brick building. Boswell headed directly for his car, while Adrienne stepped inside. The first floor was composed of administrative offices, cafeteria, library, study rooms, and recreation areas. The boys' bedrooms were located on the second floor, where they lived in groups of fifteen with houseparents. Next month she was going to be taking some of the boys to the zoo with one of the houseparents, Mr. Simmons.

At the end of the hall she peered into a small study room and wasn't surprised to find a blond-haired, freckle-faced ten-year-old. Malcolm frequently had to spend his Saturday afternoons studying because of his abysmal grades.

"Hi ya, Malcolm," she said cheerfully as she swung into the room.

"Hi." He looked up briefly from chewing his thumbnail, then gave it his complete attention again.

"How's the schoolwork coming?" She looked at the open book on his desk, then at the blank paper beside it.

" 'kay."

"What are you studying?"

"Math."

38

"Ah. I used to be pretty good in math. Maybe I could give you some help." Adrienne pulled another chair up to the low desk and smiled at Malcolm, who silently continued chewing his thumbnail. Malcolm wasn't rude or rebellious; he simply didn't seem to care about anything. He had been in Hopewell for almost a year yet had made few friends. He just kept silently to himself.

"Which problems are you supposed to be doing?" she asked, and he pointed to them.

For the next hour Adrienne worked with Malcolm on his math homework. When she left, she still felt as far from reaching him as she had the first time she'd met him. But that didn't daunt her. Some things took time.

# CHAPTER THREE

Christopher reached the station at six o'clock Monday morning. After a quick review of the day's schedule he turned his attention to other matters. He was toying with the idea of letting the newscaster, a peppy little man with a slightly nasal voice, try a spell as disc jockey. The man now spinning records had a mellow, soothing voice, and Christopher thought he'd be perfect for the news.

There was also the problem of records. When he'd begun work three weeks ago, he'd discovered the station wasn't even on the lists of some promoters to receive the latest album releases. One of his first jobs had been to send letters and make phone calls to let every record company and distributor know that he wanted copies of their newest records. He had also signed up with a second wire service for news releases, and he was trying to establish contacts at city hall so the station would get in on the ground floor of any stories that broke down there.

Things seemed to be shaping up a little. They were now receiving hot-off-the-presses albums and information about upcoming releases for the latest groups. Christopher had targeted the new image of KTOO to appeal to an audience ranging from high school age to people in their early forties. That covered the baby boom group, which had the largest population concentration. Now he intended to direct his attention toward getting new advertisers, something the station sorely needed if it was going to show an acceptable profit.

Twelve hours later, having stopped only to eat a cold sandwich for lunch, he was still at his desk. He glanced at his watch, then straightened the papers scattered across the top of his desk and rose. He had been so busy lately he had to look at his calendar to see what was on the agenda. Tonight he saw that it was a party at the mayor's house that was given annually for the local news media.

By now he knew quite a few people in the St. Louis media business, but there was one he was particularly interested in seeing. He wondered whether Adrienne Donnelly would attend and if she did whether she would come alone or with Ned. He hoped she would come alone.

For the mayor's party Adrienne chose a short jade-colored dress with a row of tiny tucks that made a frill down to her waist. She had brushed her golden red hair back from her face in casual waves. After adding a pair of gold hoops to her ears and fastening a single chain around her neck, she hurried down to meet her ride. Ned hadn't wanted to go, so Mark and Sarah were picking her up.

They came promptly at seven. Fifteen minutes later the

threesome walked through the doorway of the mayor's Tudor mansion. Mark and Sarah were soon lost in the crowd. Adrienne didn't mind. She knew almost everyone present.

The mayor himself, a trim, elegant man in his late sixties, stood beside the bar, distributing drinks. She was making her way toward the bar when she saw Christopher Ames standing near the fireplace. He looked debonair in a pale blue shirt and navy wool trousers. A houndstooth jacket was draped carelessly over the arm he held close to his body. He held a drink in his other hand and appeared to be engrossed in conversation with two other men.

At the sight of him she felt a tinge of pleasure. She would have liked to have stood there and simply watched him for a few moments, but that would have made her conspicuous. Instead, she stopped to talk to the society editor of the daily paper, then sampled hors d'oeuvres and exchanged light banter with the owner of a local television station before moving on to chat with the mayor's wife. But always, even though she deliberately kept from looking too frequently in Christopher's direction, she was aware that he was in the room.

Finally, she was standing right beside him. "Hi." She smiled at him and at the two men with him.

"Hello, Adrienne." Christopher glanced at her, then over her shoulder. "Are you alone?"

"Yes. Ned couldn't make it tonight." She felt honor-bound to mention his name just to make sure Christopher recalled there was another man in the picture. Yet if someone had asked her at that very moment what Ned looked like, she didn't think she could have described him. All she could see were eyes that were a mixture of gray and blue and a tall, virile man with luxurious black hair that showed signs of having been blown by the autumn wind. Now that she was with Christopher, Adrienne felt a surge of anticipation, although what she anticipated she couldn't say.

Christopher nodded to his companions. "Roger. Howard. I'll get back to you about the commercial." He took her arm and began steering her through the crowd. "What timing! I was hoping a beautiful damsel would come along and rescue me from those dragons."

She cast him an amused, sidelong glance that took in his square shoulders and athletic frame. "I'd say you look capable of handling things yourself. Where are we going?"

"Out. For air." He ushered her toward the front door. "If that's okay with you?" he added as an afterthought.

"Well, I suppose—"

"Good." He kept his arm anchored firmly around her as he led her outside. It was warm, almost balmy, for a September night, although the wind kicked up now and then and dusted her hair over her cheeks. The tall oaks created an overhead canopy which hid the night sky. Now that they were away from the crush of people, Adrienne thought they were just a little *too* close together. She eased herself away from him as they walked by a few people standing around in the circular drive. He let her arm go and casually slipped his hands into the pockets of his slacks. Neither said anything.

As they reached the sidewalk of the residential area, she broke the silence by asking, "How's everything going at your new job?"

"Fine," he said agreeably.

"I read about you in the paper." She slanted a sideways look up at him. No, the picture hadn't done him justice.

"Did you? I figure it's a good idea to let people know KTOO is going for a new image."

She murmured her agreement. But she knew it would take a lot more than an article in the paper to change KTOO's image. For openers Christopher would have to do something to enliven the station's dull format, and she was pretty sure he had no idea how to go about accomplishing that.

He touched the spired tops of a wrought-iron fence as they walked in front of a well-lit Georgian house. "Let's forget business for now. Tell me about yourself. Where are you from and how did you get into this line of work?"

"I'm from a small town in Illinois called Lebanon." She slowed her steps, and he dropped back to keep pace with her. "I worked at the local radio station during my college summers and liked the business." She paused to smell a late-blooming rose on a bush near the sidewalk, and he stopped beside her.

"When did you start dating Ned?"

Christopher's question caught her off guard, but Adrienne tried not to show it. "A few months ago."

"Are you two making serious plans for the future?"

"My, this conversation is taking a decidedly personal turn," she murmured.

"You can ask me some personal questions to make it even," he answered with a slow, meaningful grin.

Oh, no, she wasn't going to get drawn into that. "I already know everything about you I need to know; I read it in the paper," she said lightly and changed the subject. "Don't you think we should be getting back to the party?"

He laughed softly. "Okay, I get the point. You don't want me prying into your personal life."

"We probably should start walking back," she repeated and suited actions to words by heading back in the direction of the house.

Christopher fell into step beside her, measuring his long stride to accommodate her shorter one. "Anything in particular you're hiding, Adrienne?" he asked with a devilish grin. "Are you a Russian spy? Or maybe a man masquerading as a woman?"

She couldn't help giggling at his last question. "No, you have my word that everything about me is authentic."

"I don't suppose you'd let me verify that? . . . No? I was afraid of that," he said, sighing heavily with disappointment.

But his teasing had had the desired effect of putting her at ease again. "Tell me, do you go on like this all the time?"

"Oh, no. Usually I'm perfectly serious. But this is Monday, and Monday brings out the beast in me."

Adrienne smiled at his playful remarks and was still smiling as they approached the mayor's house. She was almost sorry to see it come into view. Christopher was an enjoyable person to be with. He made her laugh; he made her feel special. He might be blasé as far as his radio station was concerned, but with women he had some very winning ways. Just like Bobby, she reflected and moved slightly away from Christopher. If she hadn't learned anything else from her marriage, at least she'd learned to be wary of smooth-talking men.

During the following week Adrienne was kept busy at the station. September bowed to October, and the leaves began to turn beautiful shades of crimson and vermilion. Thursday night she worked late, met Ned for a quick dinner, and then returned to her condominium in Belleville, Illinois. Belleville was on the other side of the long bridge that linked Missouri to Illinois. It was dark by the time she sped up onto the bridge and drove over the dark velvet ribbon that was the Mississippi River.

Once she had arrived home, she turned on the television in the living room as she passed through on her way to her bedroom. She liked having the noise for company.

In her bedroom with lavender print wallpaper and a purple bedspread, she changed into a pair of ancient cutoff jeans and a flannel shirt her father had cast off years before. Her bare feet slapped the varnished oak floor as she returned to the living room to curl up and relax in front of the television.

The show that was on was one she had seen before, and she was leaning toward the set to change the station when a commercial came on. The upbeat voice of Johnny Burnette singing "You're Sixteen" provided background music for several teen-agers dressed in fifties clothes who frolicked around a vintage convertible at a drive-in restaurant.

"Remember what fun you used to have with KTOO?" a male announcer queried in a voice as smooth as sin. "Now you can have fun again with the new KTOO. Listen to us. We're listening to you." The words of the familiar voice simmered with provocative nuances.

The scene cut away from the girls in poodle skirts and boys in crew cuts to a cocktail party full of beautiful women with sophisticated smiles and men with knowing eyes.

Adrienne's hand strayed to her mouth, and she put her index finger over her upper lip, an unconscious gesture she often used when she was bemused or uncertain, exactly how she felt now. This was one of the slickest, most enticing ads she'd ever seen for a radio station. She only wished it had been for *her* station.

How many listeners was KXMZ going to lose to KTOO because of this commercial? she wondered, and her brow puckered at the troubling thought. Gradually, however, a smile overcame her frown, and she shook her head. She was overreacting to one exciting commercial from a down-and-out station. Okay, so it had been a good ad. Maybe it would even jog a few listeners to tune into KTOO, but until that station had something good to offer, the listeners would turn right back to their regular station—which she hoped was her own.

At least Christopher was making an effort to attract listeners, Adrienne reflected as she settled back onto the sofa and pulled her feet up under her.

She wouldn't have been honest with herself if she had denied that she felt a certain attraction for Christopher. What woman wouldn't be attracted? He was easily one of the most handsome men she'd ever known. Added to that he had the hard, lean physique of a Michelangelo statue and a personality shot full of charm. She liked the straightforward way he'd admitted changing places at the awards ceremony to be near her, liked his humor, which was sometimes accompanied by a wicked glint in those blue-gray eyes, and liked the way two brackets lifted beside his mouth to frame his smile.

Absently she smoothed her fingers through her silky hair. When they danced, she'd felt her body instinctively curving toward Christopher's, like a static-laced fabric that was governed by invisible electrical forces. A soft smile caressed her lips at the memory of the languid dances she and Christopher had shared. She had never danced with Ned like that.

Abruptly Adrienne pushed herself off the sofa and paced around the living room. Neither had she ever considered Ned in such dreamily romantic terms as she had just been thinking about Christopher. Yet Ned was the faithful, patient man who was always there when she needed a winter start for her car or help installing book-shelves. She owed Ned more loyalty than she'd shown since she'd met Christopher.

Besides, Christopher wasn't the man for her even if Ned hadn't been in her life. The simple truth was that Christopher was too much like her late husband. He made her feel dangerously impetuous. And she had to be careful of any man who so undermined her hard-won peace of mind. Men like Christopher were fun to be with, but they could break the heart of any woman who became too involved.

Still, as she'd told Kelly, no man was perfect, and Christopher did awaken a sleeping need in her that she found hard to explain. She'd felt it the night of the awards banquet when they'd danced together and again at the mayor's party when they'd traded quips during their walk. When she was with him, she felt young and carefree, like a high school girl in the throes of her first crush. But like high school crushes, she considered with adult objectivity, such feelings usually didn't last. She'd just have to wait for this one to run its course.

Over the next week Adrienne was kept busy at work. She didn't leave the station until well after seven in the evening any day until Friday. That afternoon she left at five thirty and ended up caught in worse than usual rush-hour traffic.

In fact, traffic on the I-70 bridge leading from St. Louis into Illinois and East St. Louis had ground to a complete halt. Adrienne sat in her car watching drivers drumming their fingers on the steering wheels in the cars around her. She understood their impatience; she herself was anxious to get back to her quiet condominium and a hot bubble bath.

Idly she gazed at the aging skyscrapers that flanked the river. Rising in front of the tall building and reducing them to a lesser significance with its bold, stark lines was the arch. It jutted out of the earth beside the river like a great silver horseshoe with the ends planted in the ground. On the river in front of the arch barge traffic plowed watery furrows through the Mississippi. Adrienne's gaze strayed back toward the shore where gracious old paddle-wheeler boats like the *Delta Queen* and *Robert E. Lee* were moored. A boat housing a McDonald's restaurant bobbed in the water not far away, lending a more contemporary accent to the landscape.

Behind her a car honked, and she quickly jerked her attention back to the road. Traffic had begun to crawl forward. She raised her foot off the brake, and her car began to move, too. It took more than half an hour to inch across the I-70 bridge. When she finally reached the other side, she saw that the expressway was closed and a policeman was directing cars off onto the side streets. As she steered toward the exit, Adrienne saw black smoke billowing across the expressway ahead. It was coming down the hill from a row of old brick tenements ablaze with shooting flames.

She took one look at the burning buildings, then swung her gaze resolutely away. But she could still smell the acrid scent of burning wood. Her grip automatically

50

tightened on the steering wheel, and she felt as if a cold hand had touched her shoulder. Even after five years fires still disturbed her, taking her back to that morning when she had sent Bobby off to work with a quick kiss. How could she have known then the tragedy that was to occur?

Three hours later the local sheriff had arrived at her door, hat clamped firmly in his hands, his face a stricken mask. "There's been a fire at the plant, Adrienne. I'm afraid that Bobby has been . . ."

And that was how her marriage had ended. At seventeen she had been a bride; at twenty-two she had been a widow. Bobby had been her high school sweetheart. She had been drawn to him from the start because he was so daring and exuberant. His high spirits had been infectious, and no one could make her feel as glad to be alive as he could. They'd been married right after high school graduation. Being married to him had been one glowing day after another. Adrienne hadn't really minded that he'd continued to spend evenings out drinking with the guys three years after their wedding. That was just Bobby —irrepressible and fun-loving.

Adrienne didn't know when the running around with women had started. Perhaps she hadn't wanted to know. The signs had probably been there for some time, but it wasn't until shortly before his death that she admitted to herself there were other women in Bobby's life. Initially she'd felt only shock and anger; the numbing pain had come later.

When she confronted him, he'd promised it would

51

never happen again. Even though she wanted to believe him, she'd harbored reservations she couldn't conquer. Part of her trust had died.

In a somber, more chastened frame of mind Adrienne realized if she hadn't been so wildly caught up in Bobby's spell, she would have been able to see what was going on. She had still loved him, but the pain was now as real as her love. Of course, his death had hurt her deeply, but she had also come away knowing that there could never be another Bobby in her life. From now on she would be more cautious about letting go of her feelings.

Mercifully the pain of Bobby's death had been buffered by time. In fact, sometimes now, when Adrienne looked back on her marriage, she felt as if she were looking into someone else's past. Had she really been the devil-may-care girl who'd enclosed love notes between the cheese and bologna in Bobby's sandwiches? Had she really locked him out of the house in a fight over what color to paint the bedroom? A faint smile curved her lips upward. As she looked back, that seemed such an immature thing to do, but she'd felt so *right* at the time. Funny how the years could change a person's perspective.

Red lights flashed as the cars in front of her braked. Adrienne stopped, too, again a prisoner in the clogged traffic. On any other day she might have been tapping her fingers with the grim impatience of the other drivers, but now she sat quietly, lost in her thoughts.

Her mother and Kelly still believed that she'd been hurt so badly by Bobby's betrayal and his death that she was afraid to get seriously involved with a man again.

But that wasn't true. She wasn't afraid; she just hadn't met the right man yet. Somehow she kept ending up with men who for one reason or another didn't work out. She didn't purposefully *pick* men who wouldn't make good permanent companions, as Kelly claimed; they just happened to turn out that way.

The traffic began to move faster, and Adrienne pressed down on the accelerator, feeling herself relaxing somewhat as she moved farther away from the scene of the fire and the smell of burning wood. She made a deliberate effort to take her mind off the past by looking at her surroundings.

The part of East St. Louis she was traveling through was aging and crumbling, but the Victorian brick buildings still managed to maintain a stately grace, like dowagers whose money is lost but whose pride lingers. Some of the large houses had been chopped up into apartments, and children now spilled out the front doors to play on the sidewalks.

As Adrienne continued driving, the older structures crowded close to one another gradually gave way to the suburbs. There sleek new apartments sat next to chic new shopping malls. Adrienne's own condominium was in Belleville, a pretty town bounded on the west by the heady bustle of St. Louis and on the east by tranquil farmland.

She liked living so near the country. She had grown up in a rural community only thirty miles to the east, and she still appreciated the scent of newly plowed fields and freshly cut hay. But she liked St. Louis, too, with its mixture of the old and the new. In Belleville she had the best of both worlds.

Fifteen minutes later she had reached her condominium and changed into soft green velour pants and top. She was watering her plants when someone knocked on the door. "Coming," she called.

Kelly greeted her with a conversational "What's up?" and sauntered into the living room.

"Nothing much." Adrienne put the watering can on the oak table in the dining area that separated the kitchen from the living room and settled easily into the wicker rocker to chat.

Kelly watched her slyly. "I saw your dream man on television again this morning. I think it was on the *Spirit of St. Louis Show.*"

"He's not my dream man," Adrienne protested with a laugh, then added with pretended innocence, "I assume you mean Christopher Ames."

Kelly laughed. "You know darned well who I mean. And if he's not the man of your dreams, he ought to be. When he looked out of the camera with those soulful blue eyes I felt myself start to melt."

Adrienne's smile softened. "They're blue-gray," she murmured.

Kelly continued, unhearing. "He comes across very well on television. He has presence."

"He has presence in person, too," Adrienne said in agreement.

"You like him, don't you?" Kelly's open smile invited confidences.

54

"He's nice," Adrienne said with deliberate impassiveness, then added a shrug for good measure.

Kelly laughed with knowing indulgence. "I can hear your heart going pitter-patter all the way over here."

"That might be the clock ticking that you hear," Adrienne suggested. Kelly threw a small sofa pillow at her.

"What about Ned?"

Adrienne's smile folded, and she toyed absently with the fringe around the pillow. "I don't know. We're good friends, and I don't want to lose that." Although she didn't say as much to Kelly, lately Ned had begun to seem more and more like a brother instead of a boyfriend. Her pulse didn't quicken when she was with him the way it did with . . . well, the way she would like it to.

Kelly brushed back her brown hair and changed the subject. "I've been hearing a lot about KTOO lately. Are they going to give your station a little competition?"

"I don't think so. They rarely play songs on the top ten list, and their news coverage is, frankly, quite poor. Why, they've been known to report major city news up to two days late."

"But Christopher is making himself very visible, and that's bound to draw in a bigger audience," Kelly pointed out.

"What he's doing is good public relations," Adrienne said and then added, "To tell you the truth, I'm surprised he's doing so much to promote the station. I had him figured for the laid-back kind of guy who'd drift along— you know what I mean, content with the share of the audience his station already had but making no effort to improve it." She riffled her fingers through her hair in a distracted gesture. "Even with the hype, though, I'm afraid he doesn't have a product to back him up."

"At least not yet," Kelly said, leveling a significant look at Adrienne. "But maybe he's going to change that, too."

"That thought has occurred to me," Adrienne admitted slowly. "But I just don't think he'd know how to go about it. He worked in market research in Miami, so he knows how to sell a product, but he's never worked in radio, so I doubt he knows how to *create* a product."

Kelly nodded, then added with girlish coyness, "Well, I don't care what kind of businessman he is. For my money he's still a stud."

"Down, girl," Adrienne said dryly. But she couldn't disagree with Kelly's assessment.

# CHAPTER FOUR

"Seems every time I turn on the television I find myself looking at that KTOO guy." Mark lifted the bun off his deli sandwich and added a liberal amount of horseradish mustard. He and Adrienne were sitting at a Formica table in the small canteen area in the basement of the station.

"Christopher has been getting a lot of exposure lately," Adrienne said unhappily. Recently she had seen him on two local talk shows, speaking glowingly of KTOO, smiling into the camera, and surely melting many a staunch KXMZ listener's heart.

"Course I think it's all talk," Mark continued.

"I hope so," she said. But lately she'd begun to worry that she might have underestimated Christopher. What if he really did make significant changes at KTOO? What if he wooed listeners over to his station and away from hers?

"KTOO doesn't have the money to hire really top-notch announcers," Mark added and paused to sip at his cold drink.

57

Adrienne munched silently on her sandwich. Money might be a handicap, but Christopher seemed to be working around it quite nicely at the moment. By finagling guest spots on talk shows, he was getting publicity. And he'd dredged up the money from somewhere to pay for those glossy commercials. She felt another pang of concern.

"Maybe he's really going to beef up his station and offer us some serious competition," she said morosely.

Mark lifted his shoulders indifferently. "I wouldn't worry too much about it yet. Right now KTOO is at the tail end of the ratings. Between you and me I'd be surprised if it lasts another year. Bringing Ames in is the last-ditch effort of a station that's about to go under." When she said nothing, he added, "Look at it this way: If KTOO could have afforded to hire someone competent, it would have. But it plucked some guy out of thin air. Market research, of all things," he concluded with a disgusted snort and a shake of his head.

Adrienne listened, but she wasn't thoroughly convinced, even though she wanted to be. One thing was becoming very clear, however. This man was emerging from his corner as a threat in more ways than one.

Christopher arrived late for the meeting on Wednesday night. The president of the chamber of commerce was well into an impassioned plea for innovative ways to raise money for the community chest when Christopher slipped into a seat near the back door of the conference room. His eyes moved quickly over those present until they came to rest on the woman whose red hair was tipped with gold. She glanced over her shoulder, gave him a faint smile, and turned back to the speaker.

Christopher settled back in his chair, feeling content and expectant at the same time because Adrienne was here. He'd been hoping to see her again—without Ned Riley.

While he watched her, she bent her head to whisper something to the man beside her. As she did, the overhead lights played in her hair, changing it from silk to satin and then back to silk as she straightened again. He wished he were sitting next to her. She could whisper in his ear anytime.

Adrienne Donnelly radiated a spark of life that invigorated him even from a distance. He'd never been one for fragile beauties who looked as if they should be shielded by parasols and strong men. His preference had always run to women with spirit and a sense of fun. And Adrienne definitely seemed to fit that description. From the moment he'd first seen her at the bar, his attention had been drawn to her. She had brimmed with liveliness. When something one of her companions said struck her as funny, she had laughed with such delightful abandon that he'd found himself laughing, too—and he hadn't even known what the joke was. And when she was serious, she always looked straight into the eyes of the other person and spoke with such earnest conviction that she could easily have sold snow in Alaska.

". . . so now I'll open the floor to suggestions," the chamber of commerce president concluded. Christopher forced himself to channel his thoughts back to community service for the time being. He even offered a suggestion for raising money, but as soon as the meeting was over, he made his way to Adrienne's side.

She looked up from stuffing papers into her attaché case and smiled briefly.

He studied her feminine curves and watched her supple, graceful movements with male appreciation. "If you can guess my middle name, I'll let you take me out for a drink."

She snapped the case closed. "Aloysius?"

"That's close enough. Where would you like to take me for that drink?"

Adrienne shook her head with a faint smile. "Sorry, but I've got to get home. I have a thousand things to do."

He stood directly in her way, unwilling to let her go so easily. "How about a raincheck?"

She looked up at him, and he saw a shadow of uncertainty cloud her luminous brown eyes, as if she herself weren't sure what her answer might be and she were waiting to hear her own words with the same impatient curiosity as he. Then the doubt faded. "No," she said decisively. "I don't think that would be a good idea. Excuse me." She brushed past him and headed out the door before he had a chance to say another word.

He gazed after her, brows lowered quizzically. What had he done to put her off? The last time he'd seen her, at the mayor's party, he'd had the feeling a mutual attraction was developing. Slowly he started out of the building, mulling over his latest exchange with Adrienne.

Adrienne crossed the well-lit parking lot to her car and tossed her briefcase onto the back seat. Why did Christopher have to have a voice unconsciously rich with midnight nuances that sent sensual currents through her? Why did he have to be so handsome and appealing? And what *was* his middle name anyway?

It hadn't been easy for her to turn down his invitation for a drink. But more and more, she had the uneasy feeling that getting involved with Christopher would be even more foolhardy than she had originally believed. He was more than the charming, easygoing man she had at first thought he was. But how much more? Just exactly what kind of man was Christopher?

She couldn't answer these questions. Besides, it didn't really matter what kind of man he was because she wasn't going to have further dealings with him. After sliding in behind the wheel, she turned the car key in the ignition. Nothing happened. She switched it off and tried again. Still nothing. Adrienne made several more attempts, but the engine refused to start.

Sighing in resignation, she gathered her briefcase and purse, got out of the car, and started back toward the building to phone Kelly for a ride. Tomorrow she'd have to locate a mechanic and send him out here.

"Having trouble?"

She looked up to see Christopher lounging beside a cream-colored station wagon. The letters *KTOO* were boldly emblazoned on the side of it.

She gave a resigned nod. "My car won't start. I guess the battery's dead."

"Want a lift home?"

"Well . . ." Even to her own ears her hesitation sounded ridiculous. It was one thing to refuse to have a drink with Christopher, but she would be crazy to reject his offer of help when she needed it. She grinned sheepishly. "Yes, I'd appreciate a ride."

"Good." He opened the car door for her, and she slid in. Across the hood in front of her she could see "KTOO" written in banner-high letters.

Christopher got in on the driver's side and followed the direction of her gaze. "Want to cruise by KXMZ and honk the horn?" he asked in a voice sandy with suppressed laughter.

"No, thanks." She ventured a glance at him and saw that he was smiling at her. His smile warmed her far more than she wanted it to, or should allow it to. Immediately she pivoted her head to look out the front window again. "I thought we had a very productive meeting tonight, didn't you?" she asked in her most professional voice.

"I guess so." He sounded indifferent.

Adrienne knew he wasn't particularly interested in discussing the meeting. Actually she wasn't either. But it seemed like a safe, neutral topic, so she chatted about it until they reached her building.

He parked in front of her door, switched off the ignition, and turned to her. Adrienne could feel the expectancy hanging between them on the silence. Well, she decided, there just wasn't any way *not* to invite him in without looking pretty darn rude. He had, after all, given her a ride home. It briefly occurred to her that she wouldn't mind spending a few more minutes with him before she bottled that traitorous thought.

"How about a cup of coffee?" she said.

"Sounds good." The swiftness of his reply told her he'd been waiting for the offer.

Without another word they both got out and crossed to her door. Once inside, Adrienne flipped on the lights, and Christopher looked around with frank interest, making her secretly glad she'd picked up the clutter last night.

"Nice place," he said as she moved past him toward the kitchen.

"Thanks. Do you want regular coffee or mocha?" she called from the kitchen.

"Whatever you're having."

Adrienne opted for mocha and began fixing it. In the living room she could hear Christopher moving from the bookcase to the stereo and sifting through the albums beside it. The corners of her lips tipped upward in a smile. She should have figured he was the kind of man who would make himself at home wherever he was.

"Here we are. Mocha. Tell me if it's too strong." She carried the coffee into the living room and sat down on the wicker rocker.

After slipping a record album back onto the shelf, Christopher sat down on the sofa, comfortably resting one arm over the back of it. "It's good."

63

"Thanks." She took a sip of her own coffee before saying casually, "I've been seeing KTOO's new commercials on television."

His smile unfolded slowly, beginning with a bowing of his lips and expanding to include the brackets around his mouth and the slightest hint of a dimple in his right cheek. His eyes, which were deep gray in the soft lamplight, twinkled with raffish amusement. "You don't sound very pleased by it."

She looked away from him and down to the brown liquid in her cup. "On the contrary, I think they're very good." Since he was here, she might as well ask him outright what his plans were for KTOO. "Tell me, do you have a lot of changes in mind for the station?"

"Yeah." He settled his arm more comfortably on the back of the sofa and smiled at her.

"Oh." The word was almost a sigh of disappointment. So KTOO was going to do more than just promote itself in the media. Real changes were going to be made. She frowned at the thought.

Christopher's laughter rumbled up from somewhere deep in his chest. "And I hope your station does well, too, Adrienne Donnelly."

She looked up with a guilty start. "I'm sorry. It's not that I don't want KTOO to do well. It's just that . . . well . . ."

"It's just that you want KXMZ to do *better*," he finished for her. He didn't bother to hide his amusement at her discomfiture.

She studied her fingernails. "Well, yes," she mur-

64

mured. Their eyes met, and the amusement etched in the blue-gray depths of his transmitted itself to her. She smiled and was soon laughing with him. "I sound like a great sport, don't I?" she said with a teasing smile.

"I'd be glad to play any game you want to name, Adrienne." Something shifted deep in his eyes, and the atmosphere changed between them, draping her in a net of sensual undertones.

A wave of exhilaration rose in her chest. Suddenly she felt feminine and desirable and acutely conscious of Christopher's masculinity. Her eyes slid down him, and she saw that his chest was broad beneath his tweed jacket; his thighs were columns of pure muscle that pressed against the wool fabric of his slacks; his hands were large and tanned, and she somehow knew they would feel unbearably exciting on her body. She couldn't remember the last time she had felt such a tense physical reaction to a man's presence. She couldn't remember much of anything except the tangy scent of Christopher's pine-scented cologne and the wild humming of her own pulse.

As she watched, he began to move slowly. First he set his cup on the oak coffee table in front of him. Then he grazed his fingers through his thick black hair. Finally, he rose and pulled her up from her chair.

She forgot to breathe as his head dipped toward hers and he brushed a light kiss on her lips. Then his hands came around her more firmly, resting just above her hips as he pulled her closer against him. His mouth dusted across hers a second time, and this time she parted her lips in anticipation of a more fulfilling kiss. She sensed that one was coming, but when it did, it still took her by surprise. His lips claimed hers with the intensity of a melting current swirling down from a mountain stream, drenching her thirsty mouth with a torrent of kisses.

The passionately persuasive motions of his lips on hers mesmerized her into a fevered response. She lifted herself onto her toes and circled her arms around his neck, toying with the eiderdown of the hair at the back of his neck while her whole body trembled with the singeing pleasure of his lips on hers. Her mouth clung to his more intimately as he cupped his hand around the nape of her neck and stroked with agile fingers. Desire skimmed over her body. Their kisses gave mute, eloquent testimony to the depth of their need to touch and be touched by each other.

Adrienne's sense of time eroded and crumbled, and she wasn't sure if their embrace lasted minutes or hours. But gradually common sense nudged at her, inviting her to look at the picture she presented. Here she was kissing Christopher Ames as if the world depended on it—with no thought of poor Ned *or* the fact that Christopher was her business competitor.

The moist tip of his tongue was coaxing her into a deeper kiss when she pushed him gently backward and moved away from him.

The woman in her had wanted his kisses, had perhaps invited them, but things were slipping too far out of hand. She couldn't afford to behave recklessly; she had been reckless once, and look what had happened.

The jet black brows over his smoky blue eyes contracted into a frown. "What is it? What's wrong, Adrienne?" Passion made his velvety voice husky and even more erotic.

Her unsteady breathing began to pick up the cadence of normal breathing. "Christopher, surely you can see this is wrong. I'm dating another man, and even if I weren't, we're business competitors."

He ignored the first objection and concentrated on the latter. "Business competitors?" A slow smile grazed his lips. He shook his head and smiled gently, as if she'd said something especially endearing. "Oh, Adrienne . . ."

Her name rolled off his lips and echoed in her mind like a distant waterfall, pleasant and promising. She shook her head to clear it of that image and backed away another step.

"The fact that we work at two different stations makes for a friendly rivalry; it doesn't make us sworn enemies." He hadn't moved from his place beside the wicker rocker, yet somehow the distance between them seemed to have lessened. "A hint of competition adds spice to any relationship," he continued smoothly. "Don't you ever play chess or tennis or cards with your friends?"

"Ye-es," she admitted hesitantly, "but that's for fun. It's not business."

"Competition is competition," he said reasonably.

"Yes, well—" She had a dozen good rebuttals floating in the back of her mind, but she couldn't get a grip on any of them. At the moment she was far too conscious of the changeable color of his eyes to think clearly. And she knew the emotional current charging the air between them was more the result of his provocative stance—muscular legs spread apart, hands on hips—than the job he happened to hold.

Aware that they were staring at each other for an inappropriate length of time, she tried to regain her footing by playing the polite hostess role. "Why don't we finish our coffee before it gets cold?"

His laugh dispelled the tension between them. "A woman after my own heart. Life-and-death discussions can wait, but food and drink can't, huh?"

She smiled, relieved at his light tone. "That's about the size of it," she said airily.

"Okay, if that's what you want . . ." His words trailed off as if to say it was *not* what he wanted, but he would oblige for the moment.

As they settled back into their places, Adrienne tried not to think about those moments of exhilarating abandon when he had wrapped his arms around her and she had tasted his mouth. But even as she and Christopher carried on a very sensible conversation about the tax advantages of owning a condominium, it was impossible to forget that she had been in his arms only minutes before.

When he rose to leave a few minutes later, he made it clear he too hadn't forgotten them. Neither had he been swayed by her arguments why they shouldn't date each other. "So when can we have dinner together?" he asked as he tucked his hand into the pocket of his trousers.

She shook her head. "Let's not complicate things, Christopher."

"You're right," he agreed with a ready smile. "Dinner can be complicated. Let's make it lunch. Lunch is always simpler."

Laughing in spite of herself, she continued shaking her head. "You're impossible."

He started out the door. "I'll call you, and we'll set a date."

"Don't bother!" she told him from the doorway.

Waving, he assured her, "I will."

Sighing, she closed the door and leaned back against it. Christopher was definitely of the when-they-say-no-they-mean-yes school. But he'd soon find out she wasn't playing games. Still, she felt a certain feminine satisfaction that he didn't mean to give up on her easily.

Friday afternoon Adrienne attended the board meeting of the Hopewell board of trustees. She and Boswell exchanged troubled glances as the chairman spoke. The gist of what the chairman was saying was that Hopewell was in serious financial trouble and its future was very much in doubt.

"But where would the boys go if the home were to be closed?" Adrienne asked anxiously.

"Some would be placed in state institutions, but as you know, those are already overcrowded. A good number of them would probably be returned to their homes or to foster homes."

Adrienne's frown deepened. "But if the boys' home situations had improved, they'd already have been returned there," she pointed out. "Since that hasn't happened, that means we'd be placing these boys back in the same environment they were taken out of for their own well-being."

The chairman, a jowly man with thick glasses, shook his head hopelessly. "I know, but unless we have the capital to continue operations here, there's not much we can do about that."

Adrienne doodled fretfully on her note pad as the meeting continued. Now, more than ever, she felt compelled to come up with a dazzling way to raise money for the home. She couldn't bear the thought of any of the boys being returned to unsafe homes.

After the meeting she gathered up her things and turned to Boswell with spirited resolve. "Well, we've got to do something about this."

He looked unhappy. "I agree. But the kind of money they're talking about is more than I think we could ever raise."

"We'll just have to try," she declared. "And the sooner we come up with a fund-raising plan and get it kicked off, the better."

Boswell fingered his wispy mustache. "If you're free tomorrow night, we could get together and start making plans."

"I can be free," she promised him. She had a date with Ned, but she was sure he'd understand if she canceled.

"Good. Then I'll see you tomorrow."

Adrienne remained behind after Boswell had left. She talked to the chairman and to two of the board members before dropping in for a quick visit with Malcolm. She couldn't be sure about it, but she thought he seemed glad to see her, and that lifted her spirits. It also strengthened her resolve to raise money for Hopewell. Malcolm's father had deserted him when he was just a baby, and his mother often disappeared for days, leaving the boy to fend for himself. Adrienne would hate to see him return to that uncaring environment.

## CHAPTER FIVE

Christopher called Adrienne twice over the next week. The first time he invited her out to dinner, and the second time to a play. "I'm sorry, I really can't," she said both times. She hoped he'd finally got the message and wouldn't call again. Turning him down was not an easy thing to do, and she wasn't at all sure when she might surprise herself by saying, "I'd love to go out with you, Christopher."

Late Monday afternoon, as she sat behind her cluttered desk at the radio station, her thoughts had once again strayed to the night he had taken her home and his kisses had awakened such an unabashedly fervent response from her. After having felt the firmness of his coiled muscles and the solid length of his body pressed against hers, she could attest to the fact that Christopher was all man and capable of exciting her most elemental interest.

But he also frightened her. He could hurt her. And she had learned the hard way not to trust men with bold self-assuring and winning smiles too quickly.

"Earth to Adrienne. Anyone there? Come in, please."

She looked up with a start to see Mark standing in front of her desk, one eyebrow quirked upward. Flustered, she ruffled her hands over her cranberry-colored suit. "Oh, I didn't hear you come in."

He laughed. "I don't think you would have heard the Eighty-second Airborne Division marching through your office." Dropping into a leather chair in front of her desk, he asked casually, "What's got you so preoccupied?"

"Oh, um, nothing." She randomly flipped through some papers on her desk to avoid meeting his eyes.

"It's Christopher Ames, isn't it?"

Adrienne looked at him in blank surprise. How did *he* know? She felt spots of color seeping into her cheeks as she wondered just how much of her thoughts Mark had read.

"Don't look so shocked," Mark continued. "It's natural for you to be worried about the changes Christopher is making at KTOO. I think we're all feeling a bit of pressure since he took over there."

"Yes, we are." But she knew she was feeling it in different ways from Mark and the others.

"KTOO ranked so low in the ratings that I didn't worry much to begin with." Mark raked a hand through his blond hair, and a frown darkened his features.

Adrienne felt herself tensing. Mark was in charge of advertising accounts, and he generally paid little attention to the details of running the station—unless it affected his accounts.

"Is something wrong? Are we having problems with any of our advertisers?" she asked quickly.

"Two of them have canceled," he said bluntly.

"Which two?" She held her breath as she awaited his answer. If they were two of the larger advertisers, this could cause big problems.

"Kelly's Shoe Store and Lucette Drug."

Adrienne began to breathe again. Thank God it was only two small independents. Naturally she hated to lose their business, but it wasn't the end of the world. "Did they say why they're leaving us?"

Mark nodded. "They're going to KTOO. They feel it's an up-and-coming station, and they were offered more air time for the same amount of money as they've been paying us."

"I see." She rubbed her hand across her forehead. "Well, undercutting our prices was a wise move on Christopher's part," she commented in her most fair-minded voice. Underneath, however, she didn't feel so charitable. Darn Christopher Ames! It seemed that he'd been stirring up trouble for her from the moment she'd met him. At first it had been purely personal, but now he was intruding into her professional life as well.

"Of course, losing a couple of small advertisers isn't the end of the world," Mark pointed out optimistically. "And I'll talk with some other firms I've had my eye on and see if I can sell them those time slots."

"Good idea." As he rose to go, she added, "Let's offer them our very best deal." She didn't want these new prospects to fall into Christopher's hands, too.

He grinned. "Don't worry. I intend to. Ames isn't going to get these."

After Mark had gone, Adrienne pressed her finger against her upper lip in her habitual gesture of worry. There were only three other stations in St. Louis with rock-and-roll formats. Then there was the classical music station, three country music stations, and one punk rock station. But Christopher was competing for the middle-of-the-road audience—meaning he wanted *her* station's listeners.

She straightened in her chair, imbued with resolve. Well, he wasn't going to get them! For every good strategy that he came up with to make his station more popular and profitable, she was going to counter with a better move. In fact, she was going to get to work on some ideas right now. Having opened a notebook, she began jotting down some of her ideas for station promotion. She was still at it an hour later when the phone rang.

Still writing, she picked it up and said absently, "KXMZ, Adrienne Donnelly speaking."

"It's Ned." He sounded annoyed. "Why are you still at the office? I've been here at Angelo's for half an hour. You were supposed to meet me here, remember?"

Her hand flew to her mouth. "Ohmigosh! It slipped my mind completely. Wait there! I'll be right over."

Twenty minutes later she rushed into the lobby of Angelo's Italian restaurant. Ned was standing beside a large potted plant. His brown hair had been sculpted into waves by restless fingers, and his face was lined with impatience.

"I'm sorry," she greeted him breathlessly. "I—I got caught at the office."

"Couldn't you at least have called?" he asked stiffly.

"I'm sorry. I lost track of time." It was the truth, but she knew it sounded like a limp excuse.

Neither spoke while the maître d' led them to a quiet corner of the restaurant. Adrienne unfurled the white damask napkin and placed it on her lap. When she looked up, Ned was watching her silently.

"Are you going to have the manicotti?" she asked brightly. Too brightly, she realized as soon as she'd uttered the words.

He didn't even glance at the menu. "Adrienne, is something wrong?"

She pushed her own menu aside. "Wrong? Why do you ask that?"

"Because lately, whenever we've been together, I've had the feeling you'd rather be somewhere else."

"That's not true, Ned . . ." she began, but his words rolled over hers.

"No, let me talk." He touched the gleaming silverware, arranging it just so before looking at her with a thoughtful expression. "I like you, Adrienne, but we aren't lovers, and I don't think we ever will be. We're just good friends. Maybe we should leave it at that."

She listened mutely.

Emotions fluttered around inside her like moths in a glass, but no words found their way to her lips. She felt guilty that she hadn't offered Ned more, yet she also felt a fugitive sense of relief. He was right: They weren't destined to be anything more than friends, and as long as they continued to see each other, they were keeping themselves from discovering deeper ties with other people.

His hand stilled on the silverware. "Say something, Adrienne. Do you agree with me?"

"Yes." The word was half-swallowed in the dry reaches of her throat. "Yes," she said more positively. "If we try to stretch our friendship into something it wasn't meant to be, then we'll only end up hurting each other." She smiled tentatively as the waiter appeared. "Does this mean that you'll still feed me or am I on my own?"

"I'll spring for dinner," he said with a magnanimous grin, then qualified, "As long as it doesn't cost more than a buck."

She wrinkled her nose at him, then ordered Kansas City strip. "Send me the bill," she said pertly.

He laughed. They both laughed, and Adrienne sensed that he felt as relieved as she did. She liked Ned, but he was right: There was no fire—no real romance—smoldering between them. Theirs was only a solid, comfortable friendship. And there was no reason for either of them to settle for that exclusively.

When the waiter arrived with their food, a traitorous thought struck her. Now that she was free to date other men, the only man who interested her was Christopher. Fortunately her common sense reasserted itself. It was idiotic to consider dating Christopher! Why, only an hour ago she'd been stewing about the problems he was causing her at the station. Clearly their jobs now put them in the position of rivals. Even as she thought that, however, she tried to put out of her mind an image of Christopher smiling with engaging warmth. It was plain that the traitor within herself was Christopher's ally, and she was going to have to be on guard against it.

Christopher lifted the receiver from the hook, then toyed indecisively with it. Should he call and invite Adrienne to the country club party? He'd already asked her out twice and had been turned down both times. If he were a gambling man, he'd be obliged to bet she'd turn him down this time, too. But his desire to see her was strong enough to make him willing to take that chance. Besides, balanced against those two rejections was the night he'd held her in his arms and she had answered each searing kiss with a passion equal to his own. Hardly the reaction of a woman who was completely indifferent to him.

His decision made, he dialed her home number and drummed his fingers impatiently on the desk top as he counted the rings . . . four, five. Finally, she answered.

"Hello, Adrienne. This is Christopher."

"Oh, hi." He detected a note of wariness, but it was good just to hear her voice.

"I thought if you weren't busy this Friday night, we might go out," he said.

"I'm sorry, I can't."

He didn't miss a beat. "Did I say Friday? I meant Saturday."

"I'm sorry, but no."

He was not to be daunted. "Okay, then tell me when is a good time for you. If you want to make a date between three and four A.M. on Monday, that's fine with me; I just want to see you."

He heard her draw in a deep, exasperated breath. "Christopher—"

"Can we get together and talk this over?" he said, pressing her.

"I don't see any point in that," she answered, but there was less conviction in her words now.

"What are you afraid of, Adrienne?" he asked in a quiet, soothing voice, but he knew the challenge would goad her.

"I'm not afraid of anything!"

"Good," he said cheerfully. "Then when can we get together?"

Her long-suffering sigh carried through the telephone wire, and he could have sworn he felt it whisper against his ear. "I have the distinct feeling I'm not getting through to you."

"Sometimes I'm a little thick," he admitted readily. "We'll discuss it when I see you. How about if I run over right now?" Without giving her a chance to reply, he rushed on. "Good, I'm on my way." He hung up the receiver and picked up his brown suede jacket. He slung it over his shoulder, whistling happily as he started for the door. The phone began to shrill insistently, but he ignored it.

He wasn't usually so heavy-handed in his dealings with women, but then most women didn't resist him the way

Adrienne did. And few women had caught his interest the way she had.

Kelly watched with open curiosity as Adrienne put down the receiver and muttered to herself, "Of all the stubborn, pushy men, he certainly takes the cake!"

"What's going on?"

"Christopher's coming over." Adrienne's eyes snapped, and she could feel the color settling high on her cheeks. "It would serve him right if I didn't answer the door when he gets here." But that was a bluff, and Adrienne knew it. Looking down, she began to examine critically her gray jogging suit with pink piping up the sides. "Maybe I should change clothes before he gets here," she mumbled indecisively.

"I don't think it matters what you wear if you don't answer the door," Kelly pointed out with a smirk.

"Smart aleck," Adrienne called over her shoulder as she headed toward the bedroom. There she rapidly sorted through her clothes before slipping into a pair of apricot silk slacks and an orange quilted top. She felt the excitement welling up inside her like music swelling to a crescendo as she brushed her hair and returned to the living room.

"I know I should have myself committed for letting him strong-arm me into seeing him," Adrienne said. But she spoke from a need to chatter and relieve the tense expectancy rather than from anger. "We're just going to talk, that's all, and I'm going to make it clear to him that we will never be more than professional colleagues to each other." Out of the corner of her eye she saw Kelly watching her with a troubled expression. "What's wrong?"

"Why are you so adamant about not getting involved with this guy? A few days ago I had the impression you were interested in him."

Adrienne swung her arm in a dismissing arc. "Oh, that. I wasn't thinking straight then. Besides, that was before he started making his influence felt at my station. Now he's definitely the competition."

Kelly tossed back her long brown hair. "Why do I get the feeling that that's not the whole story? Faith Turner and Mark Wilder are deejays at different stations, and they're living together. Obviously their jobs haven't interfered with their romance."

Adrienne plumped the pillows on the sofa but didn't reply.

Kelly's frown gradually resolved itself into an expression of understanding. "Ah, it's becoming clear now. You're interested in Christopher, but you're scared to death of getting to know him better. Admit it, you're afraid to let go of your feelings again, aren't you?"

Adrienne pursed her lips and rolled her eyes to the ceiling. "That's nonsense. Now will you take your high school textbook psychology and go home?"

"He makes you nervous, doesn't he?" Kelly asked with a superior smile. "He excites you."

Adrienne pointed dramatically toward the door. "Go."

Kelly stepped to the door. "I'm going, but I want a full report as soon as he leaves."

Once the door had closed, Adrienne sank into the brass and leather dining room chair and pressed her finger to her lip. Christopher did excite her, she admitted reluctantly. Even though he'd been persistent on the phone, there was no way he could force her to open the door when he arrived. If she really didn't want to see him, she didn't have to. But she did want to see him. Already she felt a breathless anticipation at the thought of gazing into his blue-gray eyes and watching his slow-dawning smile. She was like a perverse child driven to play with matches even when she knew she could get burned.

A knock sounded on the door a few moments later. Then another.

She paused to draw a deep breath, then opened the door.

"Hi." Christopher smiled down at her. His ebony hair was carefully in place, but his brown jacket was unbuttoned casually, and one hand was fitted into the pocket of his tailored slacks. He dressed well, she noted objectively, stylish without being fussy.

"Hi." Her smile flickered uncertainly. She wondered if he could sense the rush of pleasure she felt at being so close to him. To counter it, she tried to summon up the irritation she had felt when she learned KXMZ had lost clients to him. But maddeningly, the scent of his male cologne drove that thought from her mind.

He inclined his head toward the living room. "May I come in?"

Nodding, she stood back. *I'm not going to weaken and*

*fool myself into believing we could have a close relationship,* she told herself. *That's out of the question.*

He moved to the center of the living room, towering above her delicate beige sofa and providing a bold masculine contrast with the feminine bric-a-brac on her bookshelves. Shoving both hands into his pockets, he gazed beyond her. "Thanks for letting me come over."

She couldn't help grinning at that. "I wasn't sure I had a choice."

He looked around uncomfortably and pushed his hands deeper into his pockets. "Listen, Adrienne, I'm not the kind of guy who forces his way into women's lives. I'm acting this way with you only because you seem so determined to hold me at arm's length, and I don't understand why."

She closed the door and leaned against it, thankful for the impersonal support the cool wood offered her. "You work for KTOO, and I work for KXMZ. End of discussion."

He dismissed that with a shake of his head. "Something tells me that's not the full story. Is it because of Ned?"

"No. Actually I'm not dating him anymore." She kept her gaze carefully pinned on the tips of Christopher's expensive leather shoes and added, "We're friends, that's all."

It was impossible not to feel the effects of his questioning eyes as they combed over her face. Her pulse accelerated, and a blush moved up to accent her cheekbones. She was standing here saying no to Christopher, but something deep inside was crying yes. For a moment she felt an almost overwhelming impulse to press herself against his broad chest and feel the controlled strength of his arms wrapping around her. But of course, she couldn't do that.

Their gazes locked, and for several moments they watched each other solemnly. Finally, a kind of wicked merriment began to flash in his eye. "Since you and Ned are friends, I think we should be friends, too," he said in a voice as mellow as aged whiskey.

Adrienne studied him warily.

A smile creased his lips, and he slid his hands out of his pockets. "Now, why don't you offer a buddy something to drink?"

Her eyes swept over him uncertainly. Didn't he believe she meant what she'd said? Well, she decided with a repressed sigh, it was his own fault if he didn't. He'd soon find out she was serious about preventing any relationship between them from becoming anything more than casual.

"I think I have a bottle of wine open," she said and escaped to the kitchen.

By the time she returned to the living room, carrying two stemmed glasses, Christopher had settled on the sofa and was skimming the evening paper.

She handed him his drink and sank down onto the wicker rocker. There was something undeniably pleasing about a sexy, handsome man making himself so at ease on her sofa. But that man had stolen two of her station's clients in the past week—which was what she ought to be thinking about, she chided herself, instead of noticing that his legs were sinewy tapers beneath the well-cut cloth of his trousers and that his razor-cut sable hair was carefully layered in place.

He crossed one leg nonchalantly over his knee and continued reading the paper.

When he looked up and caught her studying him, he grinned and tossed the paper aside. "Sorry, a sports article just happened to catch my eye." He took a drink of wine and crossed his leg more firmly over his knee.

Adrienne shook her head in amusement. If Christopher Ames were given an inch, not only would he take a mile, she suspected, but he would also insist on having it paved as well. Still, he was going to realize he'd come up against an iron will to match his own. She hadn't gotten to be a station manager by being a pushover.

"Are you a sports fan?" he asked.

"Not really. I like to participate in things rather than watch."

His eyes lit with deep amusement. "Yes, I know exactly what you mean."

She tried to ignore the innuendo and preserve a straight face, but soon she was laughing in spite of herself. He was doing it again; he was making her feel as if she hadn't a care in the world. All that seemed important was sharing the moment with him, smiling at him, thinking about him. . . .

"I looked up Lebanon, Illinois, on the map," he said. "Isn't that where you said you lived?" At her nod, he continued. "It's not far from here, I noticed. I'll bet you go home a lot."

"Not as often as my mother would like," she confessed.

"Still, it's nice to be so close to your family."

Was it her imagination, or did he really sound wistful? "I suppose so. I haven't given it much thought. But you're closer to Houston now than you were when you lived in Miami," she pointed out. Surely he could fly home anytime he liked.

"No, I'm not." His voice was perfectly flat, and his face impassive, making it impossible for her to read his thoughts. He finished his drink and carried the glass to the kitchen. "I guess I'd better be getting on back. I don't want to wear out my welcome." Pausing beside her chair, he reached down to ruffle her hair. "See ya."

He was gone a moment later, closing the door behind him and leaving Adrienne thinking about him long after her usual bedtime.

## CHAPTER SIX

It wasn't simply because Adrienne Donnelly represented a challenge that Christopher wanted her, nor was it merely because she was an attractive woman. He also wanted her because she was warm and unpredictable, because she had a sense of style as well as a sense of fun, and because she had somehow invaded his senses and most nights he had trouble falling asleep because of tempestuous thoughts of her.

Apparently she was sleeping quite well without him, he reflected with a wry smile. She'd made it plain last night that she didn't want to be anything more than "friends." He could think of a lot better things for them to be. Sitting at his desk, oxford shirt sleeves rolled up, he tried not to dwell on them.

If it was friendship that Adrienne wanted, he was willing to begin there. But he'd learned a long time ago that patience and persistence can work wonders. He certainly wasn't giving up on becoming far more than a friend to his alluring competitor.

A knock sounded on his office door, and his secretary,

a petite redhead, breezed in. "Good news! Darrel called while you were out to say Hodgin's department stores are going to sign with us for their advertising. And," she added, holding a sheaf of papers up with a flourish, "here are the results of our latest listener poll. I think you're going to be pleased with them."

"Thanks, Dot." He beamed his pleasure. Hodgin's was the largest chain of stores in town, and its business was a real plum. Locking his hands behind his neck, he settled back with a satisfied smile as Dot closed the door behind her.

At times like this his immediate reaction was always the urge to call and tell his father of his triumphs. Ridiculous after all this time that he'd still think of calling his father—a man who had now been dead for almost twenty years. Yet he still seemed very much a part of Christopher's life.

So did his mother. Christopher never thought of her without remembering the time she'd conspired with him in the matter of the puppy. It had been brown and fuzzy, and he'd wanted it in his eight-year-old heart more than he'd ever wanted anything else in the world. The neighbors down the street were giving the puppy away, and it could be Christopher's for the asking.

Dad had said no. A final, unequivocal no. He didn't want a mutt around, chewing up the Oriental rugs and getting under the gardener's feet, he had declared.

His mother had only looked at Christopher across the dinner table and given him a small smile of reassurance.

"Don't mention it again, son," she'd cautioned after dinner.

"But, Mom, I—"

"Shh. I know how much you want the dog. But let me talk to Dad, and I'll see what I can do."

Christopher had kept his mouth shut for a whole week, a remarkable achievement considering he thought of the fuzzy brown puppy every waking moment. He ached imagining someone else taking the squirming little dog home. Every night after school he ran to the neighbors just to look and touch the wriggling animal that in his heart he considered his.

He never knew what his mother had said to change his father's mind, but it was Dad who had eventually appeared at his bedroom door, holding the squirming bundle. Dad had looked as pleased with himself as if he'd been one hundred percent behind the idea all along.

Behind his father his mother had stood, smiling softly. She had always been his ally.

Christopher had been too young when his parents had died in the crash of a private plane to understand how much that loss would change his life. His family's luxurious house with its sweeping grounds had been sold, and the money used to pay what must have been an enormous pile of debts. He had gone to live with his aunt, but she was frail and unused to children, and he'd spent much of his time with the family next door. The Evanses had a boy his age, and Christopher and Stacey Evans had soon become like brothers. He'd always felt more comfortable at Stacey's house than in his aunt's prim house with its delicate French Provincial furniture.

As a teen-ager he had gone through a rebellious stage and ran away twice. His aunt had always come down to the police station to get him out, looking at him with reproachful eyes and shaking her head. What more did he want from her? she seemed to ask. But she had never voiced her disappointment. When he was eighteen, she had died. Apparently living beyond their means had been a family trait because his aunt died as deeply in debt as his father.

Alone and broke, Christopher had set out to conquer the world, adopting a cocky air to hide his feelings of self-doubt and insecurity. His plan had been to make money. Lots of it. While he was a little short on the specific plans, he was long on dreams.

For the next four years he had worked in a series of hard, grimy jobs, beginning as an oil field roughneck in Louisiana. At the end of the four years he had saved some money, which he invested in a drilling company partnership. Unfortunately his character judgment had not yet been very well developed. His partner had skipped town with all the money, leaving behind a stack of unpaid debts, for which Christopher was now legally responsible. Bill collectors had begun calling, and they quickly grew nasty.

Christopher had kept telling himself he should declare bankruptcy or simply leave town and go somewhere to start over. But a sense of failure and defeat kept him rooted to his shabby apartment. What was the use? he'd asked himself bitterly. After four years of grueling work every dime was gone. He'd lacked the energy and will to do anything.

He didn't like to think about how long he might have continued in his depression if his old friend Stacey hadn't come by. Stacey had taken one look around Christopher's seedy apartment, pulled out some scanty details about the business failure, and pronounced, "There's something dead around here, Chris, and it seems to me you're sitting on it. Now get up off your lazy butt, and do something to get yourself out of this mess you've gotten yourself into. And if you mention the word 'bankruptcy' again, I'll knock the hell out of you."

Christopher smiled at the memory. Ah, sweet, gentle Stacey. He would have followed through on his threat, too. Stacey had always been handy with his fists. But his visit had provided the inspiration Christopher had needed. He sold his car and everything else of value that he owned, confronted all the people he owed, and negotiated payment terms. And when he was down to his last dime, he'd begun to work as a roughneck again. Only this time he took college classes at night.

Although Christopher would have denied it at the time, the experience had ultimately been good for him. It had taught him to make the most out of a bad situation. Challenges didn't daunt him now. If anything, he throve on them. He'd already been to the bottom; now he was aiming for the top.

Thoughtfully he traced his index finger along his jawline. If he had a past, so did Adrienne, and he wondered

91

what hers was. He sensed that she was afraid of becoming emotionally attached to a man, but he didn't know why. Had she been jilted in the past by someone she'd cared for, or had she never let herself get close enough to any man to risk being hurt? Whatever the explanation, he intended to get to know her well enough to break down her guard, peeling away the layers of her defenses until he was down to the vulnerable, giving woman that he sensed was the real Adrienne Donnelly.

Adrienne sat quietly watching Malcolm chew his fingernails and stare at the English book open in front of him. In the short time she'd known Malcolm, she'd discovered that he was far from stupid. He just didn't try. She wondered what it would take to motivate him.

Impulsively she leaned forward. "Malcolm, if you could have anything in the world, what would you want?"

He stared at her, blinking through the thick fringe of lashes that surrounded his wide green eyes. "Why?"

He was nothing if not cautious, Adrienne thought with a smile. "Because maybe if you work hard and bring your grades up, you'll get whatever it is you want." Who said children shouldn't be bribed?

The first look of animation she'd ever seen rippled in his eyes. "You mean you'd buy me *anything* I wanted?"

"Within reason, of course," she hastened to clarify. After all, the kid was hardly going to ask for a new Rolls-Royce, was he? She figured he'd go for a day at Six Flags amusement park or an Atari game, both of which were within her means.

"A horse," he said with deep conviction. "I'd ask for a horse."

Adrienne sank back in her chair with an inward sigh. Well, she'd asked. "A horse," she repeated. "But that wouldn't do you much good, would it? There's nowhere to keep a horse here at Hopewell," she added reasonably.

He had a quick answer. "There're some stables out west of town."

So this was more than a whim, she realized. Having a horse had evidently been a dream of his for some time.

Malcolm looked back toward the open textbook with an expression of resignation, as if to say he already knew he wasn't going to get a horse.

They both were silent for several minutes before Adrienne said, "What if I took you riding sometimes on Saturdays? Would that do?" He didn't speak. He didn't have to. She could read the answer in his eyes. No, Malcolm wanted far more than the opportunity to ride. He wanted a horse of his very own. After all, the Lone Ranger hadn't rented Silver, had he? And Adrienne suspected that was the kind of relationship Malcolm had in mind for him and his horse.

"Let me think about this," she said gently. "Meanwhile, you work on bringing your grades up. Okay?"

" 'kay."

But he was still biting his nails and dawdling over his homework when she left him. "Well, you set yourself up for that one," she told herself aloud once she was in her car. But now that the subject had been brought up, she couldn't just dismiss it. Maybe she'd come up with a solution if she gave the matter some serious thought.

Meanwhile, however, other problems temporarily put Malcolm's horse on the back burner. When she stepped into her office on Monday morning, Mark was waiting for her. His face was set in grim lines.

Reluctantly she asked the question that came immediately to mind. "Have we lost another advertising account?"

"Two."

"Big ones?"

"Medium-size."

"Oh, dear." Adrienne pressed her finger to her upper lip and sank onto her swivel chair.

"If it's any consolation, we're not the only station to be hit. I've talked to a couple of other sales managers, and they've lost accounts to KTOO, too." Mark circled to the window before adding philosophically, "Christopher Ames may be giving me some headaches, but I still have to admire him. The guy's certainly trying. And he didn't have any choice except to sell commercial time slots if he was going to make his station turn a profit."

"I know that," she said shortly. Christopher was showing himself to be a savvy, competent station manager. Grudgingly she admitted her respect for him. But that was *all* he was going to get from her. She intended to dig in now and make sure he didn't get any more accounts from *her* station.

"Mark, figure out how much we can temporarily afford to cut our margin of profit. Then call our advertisers and lower their rates to that price."

He nodded his approval. "Good idea."

That should take care of that, she reflected briskly as Mark left. She doubted Christopher could afford to match KXMZ's rates since he had less working capital to back him up. Still, she wasn't going to underestimate him a second time, not when he was showing himself to be such a formidable adversary.

Sinking back in her desk chair, she closed her eyes and pictured the last time she'd seen Christopher. Sitting on her sofa with one leg pulled casually atop his knee, he'd looked like anything but the enemy. And what was it he'd said about competition adding excitement to a relationship?

Blinking her eyes open, she straightened abruptly. What was she thinking? The battle lines were drawn as far as her station and Christopher's were concerned. He was her rival. To see the situation any other way would be to deceive herself.

Adrienne had had trouble with her car off and on since the night when it hadn't started after the chamber of commerce meeting and Christopher had taken her home. She'd had it in the shop twice, but it was still showing signs of recalcitrance. And it had picked this nippy October night to grow stubborn again.

Already she was late for a party at the home of Stan Halloway, one of her station's leading advertisers. By the time she called a cab and it arrived to pick her up it was growing embarrassingly late. To top it off, when the cab pulled up in front of Halloway's, she found she barely had money to cover the tab. The driver screeched away in an angry huff over her inadequate tip.

Outside the door of the Georgian-style mansion Adrienne paused to straighten her tulip skirt of aquamarine satin and to finger her tiny diamond earrings. She knew her hair was a cluster of wind-tossed curls, but that would have to be repaired in the powder room. It wouldn't do much good to comb it out here in the autumn wind.

She entered the lavish foyer, where crystal dripped from the chandelier like water frozen into perfect teardrops. The Oriental carpet was rich with deep reds, and the paneling was burnished mahogany.

Adrienne looked around appreciatively before slipping off to the powder room to comb her hair. The lights in the delicate silver sconces picked up the golden accents in her red hair and hinted of amber highlights in her brown eyes. After adding a fresh touch of burgundy lipstick, she headed out to join the party.

In the living room furnished with elegant Queen Anne pieces upholstered in deep blues she saw several people she knew. Adrienne chatted with a banker before moving on to talk to the owner of a computer service. After helping herself to an hors d'oeuvre, she made her way toward Halloway, the owner of Halloway record stores and a heavy KXMZ advertiser.

She had almost reached him before she noticed that the man standing beside him was Christopher. He had already seen her and was smiling urbanely at her. "Good evening, Adrienne, how charming to see you."

Her smile didn't falter even though she didn't think it was exactly charming to see *him* with one of her station's leading advertisers.

"You're looking most lovely tonight, Adrienne, my dear," Halloway said with a courtly inclination of his head.

She shifted her attention to the elderly gentleman. "Why, thank you. It's so good to see you. I'm glad you got over your bout with the flu." She smiled her most endearing smile.

Christopher intervened. "Oh, he's been over that for two weeks now, haven't you, Stan? Why, we've played golf twice since he's been over the bug."

She smiled bravely, although her spirits were sagging. "How nice." To her host, she raised her eyebrows in polite interest. "I wasn't aware you were a golfer, Mr. Halloway."

"I'm not much of one," he said demurringly. "Just putter around a bit. Say, isn't that Homer Ellis over by the fireplace? I haven't seen him in donkey's years." He patted Christopher's arm. "I want to go say a few words to the old cuss." With a nod to Adrienne, he departed.

She stood silently. So Christopher Ames was playing golf with one of her station's top advertisers. Now there was a nice depressing bit of news.

"Would you like something to drink?" Christopher asked.

"No, thanks," she said stiffly.

"Is something wrong?"

She looked him full in the face. Since he'd asked, she saw no reason not to be blunt. "You mean something *other* than the fact that you're getting ready to steal one of my station's top accounts?"

His face lightened in a smile. "Oh, I see. Don't worry. Stan Halloway is extremely loyal to KXMZ. He's not interested in advertising with us."

Adrienne felt as if a heavy load had been lifted from her shoulders, but she didn't miss the implication of his words. "Then you've already asked him?"

"Of course I have. You can't blame a man for trying," he added when her eyes began to frost over. "You would have done the same thing if you were in my position."

She probably would have, Adrienne acknowledged inwardly. Aloud she only said, "You can get me that drink now."

"What's your pleasure?"

Perhaps because she felt so relieved about the Halloway account, she answered with a coyness that surprised even her. "I don't think we should get into that. Why don't we just stick to drinks for the moment?"

His chuckle was low and appreciative. "I'm willing to accommodate in any way I can."

He left Adrienne with a lingering look of approval that set her skin tingling. She wasn't supposed to feel this way, she admonished herself futilely. Come to think of it, she shouldn't have been flirting with Christopher to begin with. She had made up her mind not to. But she was finding that making resolutions was one thing, and putting them into practice was quite another. She was a woman, after all, and she wasn't immune to expressions of masculine interest, especially when they came from a man as intriguing as Christopher.

"Here we are, Perrier water. It's what you were drinking the first night we met."

She blinked her surprise.

He flashed a brief, private smile. "Don't look so shocked. A man's bound to remember little things about a woman he's interested in."

It was more than what he said that made her feel special. It was the way he tilted his head slightly and watched her, as if he were absorbing every detail about her to examine and savor later.

A stocky man inserted himself between Christopher and Adrienne. "Hey, Chris! How've you been?"

She drifted away to speak to an acquaintance. As she circulated among the other guests, Adrienne found herself enjoying the evening more than she had expected to. Perhaps it was the stateliness of her surroundings or perhaps the fact that she was seeing old friends she hadn't seen for a while. It might have even been that she was in the room with Christopher and his occasional smiles sailed across the room to her and rested on her cheek with the gentleness of a light kiss.

At any rate, people began to leave long before she felt it was time for the party to be over. Adrienne was saying her good-byes to Halloway when it dawned on her that she didn't have enough money for a taxi home. Since she could hardly ask one of her station's most respected clients for a loan, she began glancing around for a friend to hit up.

Unfortunately almost everyone was gone except a few people she barely knew—and Christopher. There was nothing else to do but ask him. Sighing, she walked over to the marble fireplace where he stood alone.

"Um, I wonder if I could ask a favor . . ." she began. "Could you—that is, do you think you could lend me a little money?" As his eyebrows moved upward, Adrienne rushed on to explain. "Just enough for cab fare home. I'm short on cash," she ended lamely.

"I see." His mouth was level, but merriment trooped across his eyes. "What can you offer for collateral?" He made a not too subtle study of her body.

Adrienne picked up the poker from beside the fireplace and said sweetly, "I can promise not to drop this on your foot."

His laughter spilled over. "I have a better offer. I'll tell you what, I'll drive you home."

She took an instinctive step backward. "No, I'd rather you didn't."

"Why not? Do I look like a masher or something?"

"I've never seen one, so I have no idea what one looks like," she countered, hoping he mistook her fast words for a casual reply. Anyone who could have felt her hammering pulse would have known better.

Christopher put his hand firmly beneath her arm and began walking her to the door. "I'm taking you home, and that's that, so don't argue."

Since she didn't seem to have a great deal of choice,

she allowed him to escort her out of the mansion and down the circular drive to a silver Porsche. He held the door open for her, then got in behind the wheel.

During the drive back to her condominium she tried to concentrate on the winesap fall smell and the sound of leaves rustling—anything to keep from noticing that his knee was almost touching hers in the small car. The excitement he always seemed to arouse within her was building, but she wouldn't allow herself to be reckless tonight.

## CHAPTER SEVEN

When they arrived at her condominium, Adrienne threw open the car door. "Thanks so much," she said quickly. The sooner she escaped from Christopher, the better. The scent of leather and musk and the feel of his firm thigh pressing lightly against hers were awakening a sense of longing that she didn't want to feel.

"Adrienne."

The way Christopher said her name made her think of Edwardian summers and distant music. She felt as if she were being pulled back to him by something so far in her past it couldn't possibly have happened in her lifetime. Slowly she turned to face him.

He lifted a hand and stroked it across her cheek, watching her all the while with compelling intensity. A muscle flexed in his cheek. A curl tumbled forward onto her forehead. Moments passed, and they did nothing but gaze at each other. Then he bent toward her with the masculine grace of Baryshnikov. His lips anointed hers with a kiss so slight it was nothing more than the promise of a kiss.

102

Without another word he opened his door and came around to open hers. They walked to her condominium in silence. Once inside he turned her to face him. As if continuing an embrace that had been interrupted, he lowered his head again and sprinkled kisses over her cheeks. Finally, his wandering mouth came to rest on her parted lips.

It didn't occur to her not to respond. Returning his searching kiss was as natural as breathing. She coiled her arms around his neck and drew herself closer to him, tasting the dew on his lips and inhaling his musky male scent while their kiss wound on and on.

Her lips drew apart even farther as he pressed his tongue against them. A tingle of excitement spun through her as the tip of his tongue laced over hers and explored the sensitive lining and sensual recesses of her mouth. As if a low-burning flame had been turned up to high, she felt warmth sweep through her and an enticing yearning pound in her chest. Her lips grew pliant from his tender onslaught, and her body softened in feminine reply to his masculine need.

As she stretched up on tiptoe, the only thing Adrienne knew in the whole universe was the hard-lined strength of the man whose body slanted against hers. Christopher filled her senses and her mind. She would have been content to go on holding him and kissing him forever.

But a moment later he gently pushed her away. She blinked at him uncertainly. Then he bent to place one arm behind her knees and the other around her back, lifted her off her feet, and carried her into the bedroom.

There he placed her on the bed and stepped back to unbutton his shirt and shrug it off. Then he lay down beside her and claimed her mouth with unchecked furor.

Her breathing thickened as she scooped her hands through his lush black hair. Her fingers came to rest on his ear, and she felt his body grow taut. As if charged by an electrical current, he began to move again, fitting his body against hers and deepening their kiss to searching intensity.

Her hands began to rove of their own volition, going where they wished to go without consulting her mind. They skimmed over the smooth arch of his back, then rode back up on his spinal column. Every inch of him felt starkly male and tense with desire. She savored the pleasure as he stroked her with long, cool strokes from her shoulder to her hips, pausing now and again to pull her hips agreeably closer to his.

A moment later she felt him loosen the belt of her dress, then trace his hand along her back as he pulled down the zipper. In a matter of moments he had freed her of her dress, and his lips were spinning a yarn of need on hers while his hands sought beneath the filmy silk of her slip.

"Adrienne," he whispered against her throat. Then his mouth was on hers again, and his tongue danced with hers in a dizzying waltz of passion. His fingers dug into the tender flesh of her abdomen, then grew more caring as they settled on the ripe swell of her breasts. With thumb and forefinger he teased at the rosette of her nipple until her body was bow-taut and she felt something strain inside herself, desperate to be unleashed.

It had been a long time since she had experienced a man's hands shaping themselves to her body, and even longer, not since Bobby, that she had surrendered to her senses. Her body ached to join Christopher's, and her heart cried out for relief from its lonely vigil. For those few glorious moments she wanted to be part of him and feel his body moving in concert with her own. His mouth left hers and traced the delicate outline of her ear. That incited her to even greater heights, and she shifted with searching restlessness.

"Christopher." His name tumbled from her lips with no other thought than to hear it spoken aloud.

"Yes, love." The word fanned against her ear like a warm tropical breeze.

"I want you so much."

His hands gripped hers with the ferocity of a man hanging on to a life preserver. "And I want you even more," he said huskily.

But when he began to glide the slip from her, a shudder of doubt ran through her. In a moment there would be no going back. And while her body cried out for this, a corner of her mind reminded her she would have to face herself and her actions tomorrow. Wasn't this what she had feared all along? She was putting reason aside and impulsively letting the fervor of the moment sweep her along. And she more than anyone knew the folly of allowing her emotions to rule.

105

Sensing her sudden withdrawal, Christopher pushed himself up on his elbow. "What is it? What's wrong?"

"I—" She swallowed to coat the dryness of her throat. "Christopher, I don't think we should . . ."

He grew dangerously still. "Adrienne, what are you saying?"

She tried to slide from beneath him, but his body held her in an iron cage. "This isn't right."

Silence draped around them with the weight of lead. "I see," he finally said tonelessly and rolled away from her.

She pulled covers protectively up to her chin. "I'm sorry," she mumbled. "I shouldn't have let things go this far."

She heard him moving by the bedside, and then the light came on, its brightness harsh and unwelcome. Christopher was sitting on the edge of the bed, still shirtless, watching her as if she were some unusual laboratory species. "I don't understand you," he finally said.

She made a limp gesture with her hand.

"What are you so afraid of?" He disconcertedly pushed a hand through his jet black hair. "Just tell me that."

"I'm not afraid of anything," she insisted, thankful her voice didn't quaver. "I'm just being sensible. We work at competing radio stations, and it would be madness for us to—"

"That's not it!" His raised voice sliced through the room like unexpected thunder. Clenching his fists into tight balls, he gripped them atop his knees. "You're using that as an excuse, but that's not the reason."

Adrienne watched him wordlessly, silently berating herself for having got herself into this situation. She had known better, yet here she was lying in her bed with scarcely anything on while she tried to untangle her thoughts.

"Is it *me?*" he asked in a voice that was ominously quiet. "Is there something about me that bothers you?"

She bit her lip to steady it. No, it wasn't Christopher; it was her past that was getting in the way. For a woman who was heedless of consequences and willing to take chances, Christopher would be perfect. But Adrienne couldn't be so casual about relationships. Ever since she'd learned of Bobby's betrayal, she hadn't truly been able to trust any man. And it certainly wasn't easy for her to trust her dangerously sensual business competitor.

When she said nothing, he expelled a sigh, yanked up his shirt, and left the room, buttoning his shirt as he went. A moment later she heard the front door shut with controlled force.

Adrienne remained very still, as if any movement she made would shatter the calm she was trying so hard to collect. Tears grouped behind her eyelids, insisting on being recognized, but she refused to let herself cry. Once she gave into that weakness, there were too many other weaknesses she might give into—like calling Christopher and apologizing, even inviting him back.

No, it was better that she quash her feelings for Christopher before they had a chance to take root and grow. She was a competent, professional woman used to handling crises, and she would handle this one.

But the less competent, less professional person inside her knew she was also a woman who needed human warmth and comfort in her life. After years of dating men with whom she had enjoyed friendly, touch-me-not relationships, she had finally encountered a man who wanted a lot more from her. And she was terrified.

The memory of the pain she had felt the last time a man had got so close to her cut at her like shards of glass. Bobby had been the last man to possess all of her—body and spirit—and she had suffered terribly for giving all of her to him.

Because Christopher was too frustrated and angry to return to his apartment, he ended up driving aimlessly on the expressways that spiraled and corkscrewed near downtown. He had everything he needed without Adrienne Donnelly, he thought, fuming. So why was he tormenting himself with her? It was plain to the blindest idiot that she had built a wall around her that no man could penetrate. And he was a fool to keep trying.

He swept up onto an exchange and guided the car through the tentacles of the expressway, performing the intricacies of the switchbacks with grim accuracy. He'd tried to go slowly and give Adrienne time to get to know him and, he hoped, become attracted to him. He hadn't pushed too hard, had he? No, he answered his own question stoutly. The problem didn't lie with him at all. It was with her. She was a coward who was afraid of letting anyone touch the iceberg where her heart should have been. Who needed her anyway? *He* certainly didn't.

A whirling sound outside his car penetrated vaguely, but he was too engrossed in his thoughts to pay it any heed. There were lots of other fish in the sea, and he'd be a damn sight better off spending his time with one of them rather than banging his head against the wall with Adrienne.

The sound outside increased to a blare, and in his rearview mirror he caught a glimpse of a pulsating red light. He adjusted the mirror so that the light wasn't glaring in at him and drove off the expressway onto the avenue that passed in front of the arch.

A loud noise behind him jolted Christopher's attention back to his driving. It hit him all at once that the red light behind him, the squealing siren, and the patrol car were for him. "Damn!" he muttered as he pushed his foot on the brake pedal and pulled to the side of the road.

A moment later a tall, gaunt policeman was peering into his window. "Do you have any idea what speed you were doing?"

Christopher shook his head wearily.

"I clocked you at seventy," the policeman said grimly.

Christopher nodded mechanically. That was possible. Anything was possible. His mind had been on other things.

"Could I see your driver's license, please?"

Christopher found it in his wallet and handed it out the window. A moment later he silently accepted a ticket.

"Keep an eye on your speed from now on, Mr. Ames," the officer cautioned.

"Yes, sir, I will."

As Christopher continued home at a reduced speed, his bitterness toward Adrienne began to falter. When she'd kissed him, opening up to him like a buttercup seeking the sun, he'd sensed a yearning to give that was so deep it had made his throat ache. She was like a prisoner trapped by her own mind. Her instinct was to give herself to him without reservation, but her mind couldn't quite bring itself to.

But what, if anything, could he do to change her?

During the following week Adrienne threw herself into her work. By keeping ferociously busy she hoped to forget the night Christopher had aroused such passion in her. The sound of the door slamming behind him still echoed in her mind.

In the days that followed that parting she had run the gauntlet of emotions. At first she'd felt only the sharp, bleak pain of being left alone in her bedroom. Then she'd felt guilty for having led him so far only to turn him away. Eventually, however, she'd convinced herself he was also at fault. After all, she had told him over and over she didn't want to become involved with him. Why hadn't he left her alone? Didn't that make him at least partly to blame?

Still, the slamming door reverberated in her thoughts. And Christopher managed to make his presence felt in other ways. In fact, it was amazing how strongly one man could make his presence felt in a metropolitan area of two and a half million people.

At work she heard his name bandied about constantly

as tales of how he was upgrading his station and bringing in energetic new announcers circulated through the office. At home she often saw KTOO ads on television and in the newspaper.

He was turning out to be quite a different man from the one she had originally thought him to be, Adrienne considered pensively as she watered the plants in her apartment. When she first met Christopher, she had thought him handsome but without drive. Now she knew beneath the easygoing façade there breathed a man of steely determination.

With narrowed eyes, Kelly watched Adrienne pace around the apartment. "That's the third time you've watered that schefflera. You're going to drown the poor thing."

Adrienne blinked, set the watering can on the bare floor, and sighed. "I guess I wasn't paying attention."

"Still thinking about Christopher, huh?" her friend asked sympathetically. Adrienne had confided to her what had happened.

With a wordless nod Adrienne brushed her fingers across a schefflera leaf. It was beginning to seem that he was never *out* of her thoughts.

"Why don't you call him and apologize for what happened and tell him you want to see him again?" Kelly suggested.

"Because I *don't* want to see him."

"Why not?" Kelly's voice rose in exasperation. "Why don't you just let your feelings go for once and not try to keep them under such tight control?"

"You're crazy," Adrienne said. "There might be worse things than getting hurt again the way I did with Bobby, but I can't think of any offhand."

"Bobby was Bobby. This is a different man. Don't assume he's going to hurt you the same way just because he makes you feel the same." Kelly's eyes challenged her. "I admit it's a bit tricky that he's at another station, but I don't think it's an insurmountable problem."

Adrienne shook her head. "You simply don't understand." How could she when Adrienne's feelings were so complicated she herself had trouble sorting them out? She admired the way Christopher was pulling his station out of the basement, yet at the same time she resented him and felt threatened by him. Those feelings surely didn't leave any room for more tender emotions.

"Your problem is you're scared to death he *might* be the right man for you and you don't want that," Kelly said, diagnosing. "You'd rather spend your time looking for Mr. Wrong."

Adrienne shook her head with a rueful smile. "For pity's sake, Kelly. Where in the world do you get these outrageous ideas? Mr. Wrong," she repeated with a brief, mirthless laugh. Of course, she wasn't looking for Mr. Wrong. That would be ridiculous.

Kelly looked as if she meant to argue, but Adrienne cut her off. "Look, let's just drop it. I've got a lot of other things on my mind besides Christopher, you know."

Kelly propped her chin on the back of her hands and watched her curiously. "Like what?"

"Malcolm, for one thing." That much was true. While

the little boy hadn't occupied her thoughts as much as Christopher, she still puzzled over what to do about him.

"Is he the kid who wants the horse?"

"Yeah." Adrienne curled up on the sofa and brushed her index finger across her upper lip, glad of a change of subject. "I don't know anything about the price of colts, but even if I could afford one, I'm not sure it would be fair to buy one for him. I mean, what about the other boys at Hopewell? They surely want things as badly as Malcolm wants a horse, and I can't make *all* their wishes come true."

"That's true," Kelly said sagely.

"On the other hand," Adrienne continued, "Malcolm seems so down on life. Maybe if one of his dreams came true and if he had something that was truly special to him, it would put some spirit back in him."

Kelly nodded. "That's true, too."

Adrienne smiled faintly at her friend. "You're no help. Give me a concrete suggestion."

"Okay. Couldn't you find some rich old soul who'd be willing to buy Malcolm the horse?"

"I don't know who," Adrienne said frankly. "It's difficult to approach people to ask for things like that. Boswell and I are having a hard enough time coming up with ideas for raising money for the home to keep it operating without trying to come up with funds for nonnecessities like horses."

Kelly made sympathetic noises. "The fund raising's not going well either, huh?"

"No, but Boswell and I are having a meeting tomorrow

to brainstorm for some more ideas. Maybe we'll come up with something fantastic."

"Good luck."

But Adrienne's thoughts weren't fully on Hopewell, and after Kelly had left, they strayed back to Christopher. Could there possibly be any truth to what Kelly had said? Adrienne asked herself. It didn't seem logical, but then some things didn't seem to answer to logic—like the way she felt radiant and alive whenever she was with Christopher. Where was the logic in that?

The knowledge that she had been trying to stifle for the last week finally came to the forefront. She felt mind-boggling regret that she hadn't made love with Christopher. Somehow she knew it would have been the most rapturous, exquisite experience of her life. But it was complicated—too complicated for anything ever to flourish between them, she reminded herself.

## CHAPTER EIGHT

The next morning Adrienne and Boswell spent an hour discussing and rejecting ways to generate money for Hopewell. They weren't able to settle on any plan, and she was mulling the matter over when she arrived back at work. There she found a message to call Christopher.

As she read the note, her heartbeat skittered, and a rosy flush spread over her cheeks. "Call Christopher Ames." She repeated the message aloud, then walked aimlessly around her office. What did he want? Was he still angry with her over what had happened the other night? All she knew was that hearing from him had reduced her to the level of a fluttery high school sophomore.

*Call Christopher, and find out what he wants,* a stern voice from within prompted. "Yes, I will," she murmured and sat down at her desk.

As she dialed his number, she tried out appropriate openings to the conversation. "Hi," she said in her most casual voice. No, that was too personal. "Hello," she said in a deep, professional voice. No, that sounded a little too stiff.

"KTOO, Mr. Ames's office," a female voice answered.

"This is Adrienne Donnelly returning Mr. Ames's call."

Christopher came on the phone a moment later. "Hello, Adrienne." He sounded restrained, but as always there was a vibrant sensuality to his words. "How've you been?"

"Fine." She looped the curls of the phone cord around and around her finger and waited for him to continue.

"Listen, I need a favor."

"Oh? What is it?" To judge by his hesitation, he was also thinking about the other night, and it was making him as tense and ill at ease as she was.

"Dan Stahley called me. His half time show canceled on him, and he needs a last-minute replacement for tonight's game. Dan thought it might be entertaining to have teams from a couple of radio stations play against each other during half time. You know, just for fun."

Dan Stahley was the coach of the Muskrats, the local professional basketball team, and Adrienne had known him far longer than Christopher had. "I'm surprised Dan didn't call me," she said before she had a chance to think.

"Adrienne," he said soothingly, "don't feel hurt just because—"

"My feelings aren't hurt!"

A moment's uncertain silence hung over the line. Then she chuckled regretfully. "Okay, so they're a little hurt. I'm only human."

116

"Yeah, I know." Gently he said, "Adrienne, about the other night—"

It was her turn to interrupt. "Listen, I'd rather not talk about that. It's over and forgotten." Unless one counted the nights she had lain awake in her bed and remembered the cool feel of his skin and the way his lips had fitted so naturally to hers and moved with such devastating rhythm.

"All right, it's forgotten," he said crisply. "So what do you say about the half time program?"

She chewed at her bottom lip indecisively. "It's awfully short notice."

"Hey," he said with an easy laugh, "you don't need to go out and work up a training program. This is for laughs. The audience is interested in seeing some comic relief, not the Boston Celtics. Now how about it, does my station have a date with your station tonight?"

Why was she hesitating? After all, this was good publicity as well as a community-minded thing to do. True, it would involve seeing Christopher, but she was going to have to see him sooner or later anyway.

"I suppose so," she said in capitulation.

"Good. See you in the locker room. I might add I'm looking forward to that," he added with a suggestive inflection in his voice.

An unbidden smile budded on her lips. Christopher Ames was irrepressible, but darned if his playful words didn't rekindle the breathlessness she had felt lying with him on her bed. "I think it's a shade more likely you'll see me on the bench cheering for the winning team," she returned with all the severity she could muster.

He laughed. "I appreciate your support."

"Oh, brother!"

"Good-bye, Adrienne."

After she had hung up, she sat for several moments smiling and stroking her finger over her upper lip. Christopher had made her feel good. How could a man who coveted her station's audience and was stealing her station's advertisers make her feel good? she asked herself, and immediately the smile wilted.

Recruiting a team wasn't difficult for Adrienne. None of the deejays was shy, and they relished the chance to show themselves to a public that knew them only by their voices.

Just how enthused they were became evident that night, when Adrienne arrived at the gymnasium, wearing her old high school cheerleader outfit and feeling a little self-conscious in it until she saw how outlandish the other outfits were. William, who did the late-night show, was dressed as Superman. Gregg wore a cap and gown; his number was pi. Mark, number 2½, wore a pink tutu, and Joy, the peppy female disc jockey, arrived in a bear costume. They all stood around the sidelines, being conspicuous, as the first half of the game got under way.

And then there was Christopher. He wasn't a player, but he had come to cheer in style—1920s style. His varsity sweater was yellowed with age and full of holes. His raccoon coat was moth-eaten, and his raven hair was parted in the middle and slicked down with oil.

Adrienne watched him from her seat on the bench, his ready smile and quick laughter distracting her from the game. Even in that absurd outfit her blood stirred as it had not done since the night she'd felt his bare skin pressed against hers. *Stop it,* she scolded herself, and busied herself straightening her red sweater and candy-striped skirt.

A moment later Christopher joined her on the bench. "Well, hello."

She tried for a nonchalant smile, but the smile deepened of its own accord as the ridiculous raccoon coat brushed against her. "Hi, Christopher."

A gleam of male appreciation dawned in his eyes as he took in her outfit. His gaze came to rest at the middle of her thigh where the skirt ended. "What's this? Are you going to try to distract my team's superstars by shamelessly flaunting your legs?"

She looked down at the sinuous curves of her legs and tried not to be pleased by his approval. But she couldn't help remembering that he'd been admiring her legs that first time they'd met. She wondered if he was thinking the same thing.

"Got any goldfish on you?" he asked. The twinkle in his eyes was irresistible.

"Not at the moment."

Just then the crowd surged to their feet around Christopher and Adrienne, exuberant over some action on the court she had not seen.

"We're missing the game," she pointed out.

"So we are."

119

She was glad to have an excuse to focus her eyes elsewhere. Even in a mothy coat Christopher upset her equilibrium. Fortunately she soon became caught up in the playing, although she did notice Christopher as her head swiveled back and forth, watching the teams move from one end of the court to the other.

The home team scored another two points, and she was on her feet again, cheering. Then it was half time, and the KTOO and KXMZ "teams" took the court.

"There goes the pride of KTOO," Christopher said, hand flung over heart.

Adrienne fluttered her pompoms in his face.

It soon became apparent the teams had little appreciation of the finer points of basketball. Instead of a tip-off, they flipped a coin to see who got the basketball. KTOO won and rolled the ball down the floor like a bowling ball. KXMZ recovered it and used it as a soccer ball.

Adrienne cheered wildly when Mark stood on Lionel's shoulders to put the ball through the net. The game ended when KXMZ's lanky sportscaster kidnapped KTOO's tiny center and the other players chased them out of the gym.

Christopher grinned at her. "Who won?"

She laughed. "I'm not sure, but both teams played fine games." Her liveliness subsided as she became aware that his smile had segued into something more private. Beneath the gym lights his eyes were heather blue, and they were fixed on her in a way that made her breath jam.

The moment was broken when Marty, the burly assistant coach, appeared beside them and began talking

120

about the ball game—the real one. After a few moments of lamenting the referee's appalling eyesight, at least on the opponent's end of the court, he turned to Adrienne and continued. "I hear you're helping raise money for Hopewell. I do a little volunteer coaching out there myself."

Christopher looked from one to the other. "Hopewell?"

"Boys' home," Marty explained out of the side of his mouth and continued to Adrienne. "So you're taking some of the kids to the zoo over Veterans' Day weekend?" Snorting in wry amusement, he shook his head. "Lots of luck. The missus and I took 'em to the fair once, and the little buggers ran amuck." He glanced over his shoulder toward the players. "Oops! Gotta go. See you-all around."

Adrienne was aware of Christopher's curious eyes on her as the play resumed. During the next time out he turned to her. "Is this trip to the zoo a private party, or can anyone go along?"

She fingered her pompoms and parried the question. "Why do you ask?"

"Because I'd like to go," he said simply.

She bit back a sigh. Why couldn't he understand that the less she saw of him, the easier she would feel?

He must have read her hesitation and guessed the reason for it. "Listen, we agreed we were going to be friends, remember? As a friend I'd like to help. From what Marty said, you may need a hand."

She hesitated. "Wel-l-l-l." He was probably right about

their needing a hand. Adrienne rippled her shoulders in a shrug. "I suppose so. Why not?"

Christopher returned home, pondering the night's events. It had been worth wearing his smelly old raccoon coat and lacquering his hair just to see the amusement flash in Adrienne's eyes.

*Don't push her* he'd had to keep reminding himself. And he hadn't.

But he didn't know how much longer he could curb his impatience. The radio station took up a good deal of his attention, but during the moments that were his own he wanted someone special to share them with. And Adrienne was special to him. Her laughter, her femininity, her wit, and her intelligence all combined to make her a unique and captivating woman. He never felt lonely when he was with her or as if he were missing some essential part of himself.

After stripping off his clothes, he stepped into the shower and began washing the oil from his hair.

If only he were important to her. While he could be dogged in pursuit of something he really wanted, he had an ego, too, and it was getting a little battered by Adrienne's constant rejections. What was it that caused her to keep her distance? Was there a man in her past that she still loved? An old wound that had never healed?

"She's driving me crazy," he growled from beneath the water as he lathered his hair.

He wished she were with him now. He longed to feast in those big brown eyes, and he wanted to stroke those

122

sensual lips until they divulged her secret. If she were here, he could satisfy the ache he sometimes felt to trace his hands over the downy contours of her cheeks and sift his fingers through the richness of her soft red hair.

At least they would be going to the zoo together, he thought to console himself. Granted, with a dozen boys milling around them, it probably wouldn't be the most romantic encounter he'd ever had. But at least he would be with her.

The week passed, but Christopher didn't call Adrienne —*all to the good,* she told herself. The November winds shook the remaining leaves from the trees and blew a cold wind off the river.

Saturday afternoon Adrienne and Boswell met at Hopewell in the empty conference room to kick around some more fund-raising ideas. As she sat at the table, she pushed back the golden red strands of hair slipping down over her forehead. Boswell sat across from her with his tie loosened and his shirt rumpled. They had been sitting at the conference table for two hours now, racking their brains for an idea that was innovative and would bring in the kind of money they needed for the home.

"What about raffling off something really big? Say, a new car?" Boswell said wearily.

Adrienne shook her head. "Unless we could get someone to donate the cost of printing the tickets, that's expensive. Then there's the problem of finding enough people to go out and sell the tickets. And that's *if* we could get someone to donate a car."

Nodding dejectedly, Boswell sank back into silence.

During the past hour they had explored and rejected dozens of ways of raising money. Some ideas would cost almost as much to implement as the revenue they would raise. Some had been used in the past and had not proved successful. Another complicating factor was that certain fund raisers were annual events of other charity groups, such as the Society Horse Show, Policeman's Ball, and the telethon for cerebral palsy.

"I keep thinking there must be something terrific I'm overlooking," Adrienne mumbled.

"I know what you mean."

"We can get all the free advertising time we want," she said unnecessarily. "But we've got to come up with something sensational to advertise to raise the kind of money we need."

"Yeah." Boswell stroked at his mustache and looked thoughtful. Suddenly his eyes fell on the wall clock, and he stiffened. "Uh-oh! I have an appointment in a few minutes." Rising, he jammed papers into his briefcase.

"Let's both keep thinking about this. I have a feeling one of us is going to have an inspiration."

"Call me when it happens," he said dryly.

After he had left, she strolled idly into the television room. Malcolm was sitting in the corner, and after exchanging a few words with the other boys, she crossed to him. "How's it going, fella? Are you looking forward to the trip to the zoo tomorrow?"

He turned clear green eyes up at her, and she could see

every freckle on his face. He looked so young, she thought with a pang.

"I have something to show you," he said, and she recognized an undercurrent of excitement in his words.

"Oh?"

"Wait here," he said and dashed from the room.

She heard scurrying footsteps. Then he bounded back into the room, carrying three sheets of smudged paper. "See. As. I got As on all of them." He handed her the papers. "Well, one's an A minus," he conceded. "But that's good enough, isn't it?"

"That's very good!" she exclaimed as she leafed from one paper to the next. While she looked at the papers, she became aware that Malcolm was watching her expectantly and then it hit her what he meant by "good enough." *Oh, dear,* she thought faintly. She had not spoken with Malcolm again about the horse. Did he think they'd reached an agreement that if he improved his grades, he would get the horse?

"Malcolm," she began carefully, "I'm not sure—"

A ruckus erupted on the other side of the room over the choice of television stations. Adrienne waited for it to subside while she tried to think of what to say. She finally settled on the truth. "Malcolm, I don't think I can afford to buy you a horse. Besides, it wouldn't be fair to the other boys if I did," she explained gently.

For a moment he watched her steadily. Then he reclaimed the papers and said without expression, "That's 'kay."

"I'm very pleased about your schoolwork," she pursued with an artificially bright smile.

"Yeah." He looked downward and dug at the frayed carpet with the toe of a shoe. "I guess I'd better get upstairs and make my bed."

"I'll see you tomorrow. I know we're going to have a lot of fun at the zoo," she said in a weak effort to inject a note of cheer into the dismal atmosphere.

"Yeah." He was gone a moment later, leaving Adrienne feeling like a heartless, insensitive heel. Absently, without any clear idea of where she was going, she wandered out to her car, head bent, feet dragging. Poor Malcolm. She understood the letdown he must feel about the horse. But what could she do?

The next day Adrienne arrived back at Hopewell shortly after noon. She was determined to appear cheerful for the sake of the other boys. When she had a chance, she'd get Malcolm off by himself and offer to buy him a toy. A dozen exuberant boys were in the process of boarding the orange minischool bus when she reached it.

"I get the back seat!" one shouted.

"I called it yesterday, you turkey."

Christopher was already on board, and she smiled at him as she stepped up onto the bus. "Aren't they sweet?" she asked with gentle mockery.

"I'd say they're about typical for nine- and ten-year-olds." He was wearing well-worn jeans and a T-shirt that read "Honcho." "For the benefit of the boys," he explained with a grin as her eyes skimmed over the red lettering. "So they'll know who's boss."

She smirked. "Wait until you've spent half an hour with them. Then *you'll* know who's boss." As she spoke, her eyes scanned the interior of the bus. "Where's Malcolm?" she asked Jon, the towheaded boy closest to her.

"He ain't goin'." Jon unwrapped a stick of gum and shoved it into his mouth.

"Not going? Why?" she asked.

"I dunno. I think he's sick or somethin'."

"Malcolm didn't wanna come," someone hollered from the back of the bus.

Adrienne tried to conceal her regret. He was still upset about the horse, she was sure.

The driver, a thin man with a face creased into what looked like a perpetual smile, boarded the bus along with Mr. Simmons, the houseparent, who counted heads. "I guess that's it," he announced as he closed the door.

Mr. Simmons gave a brief lecture about remaining seated and holding down the noise. It didn't appear to have had much effect, Adrienne reflected as the trip got under way and the chatter of voices swiftly rose to a deafening din. She couldn't have talked to Christopher if she'd wanted to, but she wasn't much in a mood for talking. That Malcolm hadn't come worried her, but she knew she couldn't dwell on it today. There were other boys who had come, and she had to make sure they had fun.

They reached the zoo half an hour later. Mr. Simmons rose and waved the boys to silence. "Okay. Half of you kids are going with me, and the other half will go with Miss Donnelly and her friend. I'll read out the names."

When it was all sorted out, Adrienne and Christopher found themselves in charge of Jon; a chubby boy named Micah; a dark-skinned boy named Raoul; Kenny, the ballplayer; Jeremy; and Lamont.

"I want to see the tigers first," Jon declared.

"Aw, tigers are stupid. Let's get some candy."

Raoul tugged on Adrienne's arm. "Will you buy me something?"

"No. Now here's what we're going to do." She held the map aloft. "We'll start by—"

Raoul wasn't taking his dismissal so easily. "Why won't you buy me something?" His voice was acquiring a whining edge.

Adrienne looked up to see Christopher leaning against a signpost and watching with vast, unconcealed amusement. Around her the boys were voicing grumblings, pleas, and suggestions.

"Okay, honcho," she called to Christopher, "now's the time to show them who's boss."

He sauntered over to her. "Put a lid on it, guys," he said firmly.

There must have been enough authority in his voice to convince the boys he meant business, for their voices soon dwindled away. When all were silent, Christopher continued, "Now we're going to start at Big Cat Country."

"Why?" Jon asked.

"Because I said so, and I'm the honcho. See." He drew his finger beneath the red lettering on his T-shirt.

Raoul snickered. "What are we?"

Christopher didn't miss a beat. "You're the ranch hands."

Kenny pointed to Adrienne. "What's she?"

Amusement glimmered in the smoky blue eyes. "She's the crotchety schoolmarm."

The boys hooted. Adrienne swatted Christopher's arm with the map. "Thanks a lot! Well, are we going to stand here all day, or are we going to see the animals?"

"We're going to see the animals," Christopher said firmly. "What's first, men?"

"Big Cat Country," five of them chanted.

"I want ice cream." Raoul was the lone dissenter.

Adrienne fell into step beside Christopher as they set off. The zoo was set in an area of bluffs, woods, and glades with the animals living in naturalistic settings. It was great for the animals, Adrienne conceded after the first hour, but it made for a lot of walking.

Except for the fact that her tennis shoe was rubbing slightly at the back of her heel, she didn't really mind. And the boys were enjoying themselves immensely. They indulged in a few mild curse words and scuffled a bit, but she thought that was showing off for Christopher's benefit. They all wanted to impress him, she recognized, but that was natural for boys their age, especially boys who didn't have fathers they could look up to and admire. And Christopher was, after all, an impressive figure.

While they might not share her female appreciation of

129

his tanned good looks, Adrienne could see the boys were in awe of his athletic build.

Gradually she realized there was something else taking place between Christopher and the boys that she couldn't quite put her finger on. In some indefinable way he seemed to be a kindred spirit to them and instinctively to understand their feelings. When Kenny paused to watch a lioness with her two cubs, Christopher stopped beside him and put his hand on the boy's shoulder. Both were silent, and for a moment she was surprised by the lack of gibing. Then she saw the wistful expression on Kenny's face as the cubs snuggled against their mother. *He wishes he had that kind of motherly caring in his own life,* Adrienne realized with a start. And it was even more of a surprise to acknowledge that Christopher had understood that instantly.

Christopher nudged Kenny. "Come on, fella," he said gently, "let's go see about some ice cream."

The others fell in excitedly. "Good! I'm *starving!*" Raoul said.

At the refreshment stand, while the boys agonized over flavors, Adrienne sat down beside Christopher at a picnic table.

"I'm glad you came today," she said quietly.

"Thanks." He took her hand.

Adrienne had a funny feeling that Christopher was as much in need of someone to touch as Kenny had been moments before. At any rate she didn't draw her hand away. She felt she was seeing a side of him that she'd never seen before, one that he didn't show to many people. He could be vulnerable, she realized, and wondered what it was about these boys that had brought out that side of him.

"I get to sit by Christopher!" Jon said in a shrill voice.

"I do!" Raoul yelled.

"I certainly am popular today," Adrienne said with mock dismay. "No one's fighting to sit next to me."

"It's nothing personal, but well, you're a girl," Christopher explained to her as kindly as possible before sliding away from her to make room on either side of him for the two boys.

She smiled. "There isn't much I can do to change that, is there?"

His eyes swept over her before he said simply, "I wouldn't want you to."

Had they been alone, she couldn't have said what might have followed that remark. He looked as if he'd have liked very much to kiss her. She'd have liked it, too. In fact, just basking in the warmth of his smile was awakening longings that had no place in a public zoo.

Jeremy broke the spell between them. "Why are you two staring at each other? And when are we going to the Children's Zoo?"

"You're right, Jeremy. Seeing the Children's Zoo is the most important thing I can think of doing right now." But his eyes lingered on Adrienne.

## CHAPTER NINE

Adrienne was exhausted but content by the time the bus finally arrived back at Hopewell. She watched the boys trundle off the bus and up the steps of the home and waved good-bye to them before turning back to Christopher.

She and Christopher had spent the day in an undeclared truce. He hadn't pressed to see her again, and she hadn't mentioned the competitive nature of their jobs once. After the easy camaraderie they had shared she was reluctant to see the day end.

To judge from the way Christopher was looking at her, he felt the same way. "It's almost six o'clock, and you haven't eaten dinner yet," he said. "Why don't we go get something?"

She hesitated. "I've already got something fixed at home. I put some stew in the crockpot this morning before I left," she explained.

"You could invite me to share it," he suggested.

She chewed at her lower lip indecisively. She didn't deny she'd enjoyed the day with him, but how wise was it to invite him back to her house? "I didn't make much . . ." she began.

"That's okay. We'll just add some water," he said glibly, smiling. "I'll meet you at your place in twenty minutes." He headed across the parking lot toward his car.

"I didn't invite you," she said, torn between amusement and exasperation.

"Twenty minutes!" he called as he got into his Porsche.

Adrienne shook her head and opened the door of her car. You could say a lot of things about Christopher, but you couldn't say he lacked persistence. Her wry expression softened as she recalled the other side of Christopher that she had seen today. He hadn't treated the boys with pity or acted overly protective toward them, but she had detected a quiet sense of caring flowing like a current beneath his teasing. What had happened in his life to make him so sensitive to these boys? she wondered.

It was probably better that she didn't know, she told herself. His past didn't concern her. She didn't want to get any closer to Christopher than she already was. But her feelings were at war with her logic.

By the time she arrived at her condominium Christopher was waiting outside her door. His hands were thrust into the back pockets of his jeans, and she couldn't help noticing he even had an appealing way of slouching that showed his lean physique to maximum advantage.

She unlocked the door and pushed it open. "Come on in."

Christopher followed her into the kitchen and watched her as she checked the stew. "Do you want me to slice some bread or make a salad?" he offered.

"You can set the table. The dishes are in the cabinet by the refrigerator."

Ten minutes later dinner was on the table. The addition of cheese and crackers and a plate of fruit helped make up for the meager portions of stew.

As they settled down across from each other at the table, she asked conversationally, "Have you gotten to see much of St. Louis?" That seemed a safe, impersonal subject.

"Yep." His knuckles brushed against the back of her hand as they both reached for cheese at the same time. Adrienne couldn't have sworn it, but she thought the touch was deliberate. "Last weekend I gave myself the grand tour," he continued.

"Oh? What'd you see?"

"I saw it all," he said expansively. "The arch, the Cahokia Mounds, the old courthouse, the museum, and the Anheuser-Busch Clydesdales. Those are big horses," he commented.

"Yes, they are," she murmured, but the mention of horses had made her think of Malcolm. Poor kid. Had he stayed in his room all day grief-stricken because the As had not gotten him the horse he longed for? It didn't seem fair that he would have tried so hard and then been deprived of his reward.

Christopher tilted his head to one side quizzically. "Is something wrong?"

"No, nothing." She brushed aside the question. She didn't want to talk about Malcolm, so she directed the subject back to the sites of St. Louis. They finished their meal and moved into the living room to drink their coffee. She sat on the sofa; he, on the chair. As she sipped the hot coffee, he told her about riding the egg-shaped elevators to the top of the 630-foot metal arch and looking out from the top onto St. Louis and the farmlands for miles beyond.

The more he talked, the more engrossed Christopher became in his subject. She watched him stretch out his hands to describe the level farmland and then bring his fingers close together to show how the toy-size boats going down the river had looked from the top of the arch.

Then he talked about the museum on the ground beween the two legs of the arch, about the Anheuser-Busch brewery tour and the beers he'd sampled in the hospitality room. Using his hands again, he described the Cahokia Mounds, a truncated pyramid built by prehistoric Indians.

As she listened, Adrienne felt some of the tension about Malcolm drop away from her. Having slipped out of her shoes, she curled her bare toes over the white area rug and relaxed even further.

"Its base covered more than the thirteen-acre base of the Great Pyramid of Cheops. The Indians who built the mounds—" He broke off with a sheepish laugh. "I'm sorry. I didn't mean to go on and on. You must be bored to death."

She shook her head. "I'm not bored. I'm enjoying it."

"You sure?" He was watching her again in the same intense, yearning way he had looked at her at the zoo when he'd held her hand.

At first she couldn't meet his gaze directly and looked away. But something drew her back. On the surface Christopher seemed a self-assured, confident man, but she thought she glimpsed, hidden in the depths of his eyes, a need so raw he was at pains to keep it concealed. Something about that expression made her want to reach out to him and soothe away his troubles.

Slowly he rose. "I've taken up enough of your time today. I'd better go now."

Adrienne looked down at her empty cup and ran the tip of her finger around its rim. She didn't want him to leave. All the things that had stood between them suddenly seemed of no importance. What mattered was that she wanted to be with Christopher right now.

She'd kept her heart wrapped in tissue paper for too long, like a fragile piece of china stored but never used. Kelly was right; she had been afraid to let this feeling happen. But with Christopher her heart had made its own choice, and she felt an invisible bond joining them together. If he left now, she knew he would be taking part of her with him.

And why was he leaving anyway? Because she was afraid to risk getting involved with a man who inspired such strong feelings in her? She'd feared all along that once she'd admitted her attraction, she'd be helpless, so she had set up arbitrary rules that made no sense even to her anymore. How could she limit Christopher and her to friendship when she felt a kinship for him beyond any mere friendship? She could no more contain the way she felt for him than she could prevent a hurricane or an eclipse.

The fact that he was a competitor didn't seem to matter now. She had seen a different side of him at the zoo, and she knew he could be sensitive and caring. And wasn't that what she had always wanted in a man?

Feeling exposed and uncertain, she got to her feet. "Don't go."

His brows inverted into a questioning frown, as if he were afraid he had misunderstood what she'd said.

She held a hand toward him, palm upward. "I want to be with you, Christopher."

He walked to her side and tilted her face up to his. "Are you sure, Adrienne? I can't start something we can't finish. I can't do that again."

No, and neither could she. Nodding, she brushed a finger over his lips, then brought her other hand up and put a hand on either side of his face. The slight prickliness where he had shaved grazed her palms, but the tips of her fingers touched the smooth planes of his cheekbones. It felt wonderful just to touch him.

His lips came down to hers with sweet slowness, hovering about her mouth like a butterfly over a rose petal. She pressed her hands against his chest and felt the strong signal of his heart drumming. Then his lips covered hers in a kiss sharp with desire.

Adrienne drank in his kisses as if she were drawing sustenance from him. His hands wandered through her hair, but he continued to exact full payment in his kisses, demanding and urging and fulfilling all at the same time.

She let her hands glide down to his abdomen, and he murmured his approval. They kissed and caressed and reveled in each other's touch. She lost first her blouse and then her slacks to his marauding hands. And without her clothes on his touch was even more exquisite on her body. His fingers searched out the vulnerable softness of inner thighs and swollen breasts.

He pushed a chair out of the way and pulled her to the floor beside him. The white rug cupped her back in softness, making a beautiful contrast with his lean hardness.

Then he pulled out of his clothes and tossed them away in untidy balls, heedless of where they landed or of wrinkles, intent only on her.

Christopher's searching kisses pulled her into the vortex of his passion, but the soft persuasions of his lips didn't deter the skill of his hands. They brushed through her hair and stroked the bare lines of her back, waiting to explore more intimately until her body arched up to him in open invitation. And when he finally touched her satiny woman's flesh, pleasure ran through her like quicksilver. She sent her hands on their own investigation and felt him respond with a gasp of pleasure and inarticulate moans.

Their delving kisses and the slow motions of their hands were only a beautiful prelude to the moments to come. They both knew that. But it was still a treasure of almost unbearable dimensions when her body opened up to accept his and masculine angles fitted themselves to her feminine curves until they were together on an odyssey of pleasure. His body moved for both of them, beginning with a gentle sway but leading up to a more urgent tempo that would satisfy the craving they both felt. And all the while his lips tempted her deeper and deeper into the realm of his kisses.

He was moving more intently now, and her body had joined in the compelling cadence. She felt heat invading her body, beginning as a sprinkling of warmth at her fingertips but growing to a fire that raged from the very core where their bodies joined. She felt completely enmeshed with him, belonging to him and wanting to bind him forever to her. Then, for one blinding second, a sensation that defied all description ricocheted through her body. She knew only that she was touching heaven and confronting bliss in such stunning force that it would have come near the edge of pain if it hadn't been so sweet.

Then slowly she began to return to reality. She could hear Christopher's tearing breaths and wrapped her arms around him, burying her face against his chest.

Several moments later he said, "Adrienne?"

"Hmmm?"

"Thank you." A wealth of emotions was expressed in those simple words.

She raised her face to his and looked into eyes that were midnight blue with the remnants of passion. She was too moved to think of an answer, so she only brushed his flushed cheek with the back of her hand and kissed him softly. Then she turned off the light and they lay down together on the furry rug.

When she awoke the next morning, Christopher was still lying beside her. His face was pressed into the white fur, and one arm was flung out to his side.

Her first reaction at seeing him was unchecked delight. She felt far too happy to lie silently beside him while he slept.

"Wake up," she cooed into his ear and then tickled at his ribs.

He bolted upright. "What the—"

"Hi." She smiled directly into his face and gloried in the look of slow pleasure that dawned in his eyes.

"Good morning," he said huskily. "Come 'ere."

She snuggled down with her cheek against his chest and blew on the little wisps of black hair that grew there. "G'morning." Still nuzzling against the solid wall of his chest, she said, "So tell me, what's your middle name?"

She felt the delightful vibration in his chest when he laughed. "Is that why you enticed me to spend the night? Just to ferret out secrets about me?"

"Mmmhmmm," she said languidly. "So what is it?"

"Allen."

"Allen," she repeated and raised herself up on one elbow to survey him critically. "I'm not sure you look like an Allen. I picture Allens as being studious and a little backward." He certainly hadn't been backward last night!

"It was my mother's maiden name," he explained.

"But if you don't like it, I'll see what I can do about having it changed."

She grinned at him. "I wouldn't want to start any family feuds."

He fitted an arm loosely around her waist and slid his other hand behind his head so that he was lying looking up at the ceiling. "There's no family left to feud with. My parents and my only aunt are dead."

"Oh." Adrienne felt that she had clumsily stumbled into a sensitive area. "How long have your parents been dead?" she asked carefully.

"Since I was ten," he said in a voice curiously devoid of feeling.

She thought immediately of Malcolm. He was ten now. Although his parents were still alive, he was essentially alone in the world, and that struck her as an awesome burden for one so young. "That must have been rough." She peeked at him cautiously, prepared to drop the subject if Christopher seemed reluctant to talk.

"It had its bad moments," he said obliquely.

She delicately touched his taut stomach. "Do you mind talking about it?"

"Not with you," he said quietly. She tilted her face up to his and saw that he was watching her with a heart-stoppingly tender expression. His mouth quirked up into a one-sided grin, and he gave her a quick kiss on the nose. "Don't look so concerned. You don't have to worry about me. I'm a big boy; I get by."

Yes, he got by, but Adrienne better understood now his instant kinship with the boys from Hopewell. He knew

141

what it was like to be without close family or someone who cared.

Rising, he began slipping into his jeans. "I'm starving. What are you going to feed me for breakfast?"

"I always have cold cereal." She got up, too, and went into the bedroom to get a robe. On the way into the kitchen she tied her filmy robe about her.

"Cold cereal! You've got to be kidding." His voice came out muffled from the depths of the refrigerator. "What? No eggs? No bacon?"

"Eggs have cholesterol, and bacon has nitrite," she said virtuously.

He emerged to look at her in horror. "You aren't a health nut, are you?"

Adrienne laughed. "Not really. The truth is I usually keep bacon and eggs, but I haven't been to the store in a while."

"That's a relief. I enjoy my junk food too much to give it up—even for you." He pulled her into his arms and nibbled at her ear. "Well," he decided as he nuzzled lower, "I might give it up for you."

"I thought your appetite was for food," she said reprovingly even as her body swayed into his caressing hands.

He pulled back briskly and gave her a quick, decisive kiss on the mouth. "Right. There'll be time for other things later."

Over hot oatmeal and sausage she and Christopher chatted comfortably. After he had finished his orange juice, he settled his elbows on the table and watched her.

Adrienne soon became aware his gaze had dropped from her face and was directed to the cleavage exposed in the deep V of the gown. Automatically she raised her hands to draw the gown closed.

He laughed with happy exuberance and brushed her hands away. "Don't go shy on me now. What you've got is too perfect to hide." Pushing back his chair, he drew her out of hers. "Much too perfect," he added in a thickening voice that raised her body temperature by several degrees. His hands felt strong and solid as they encircled her body. "I think we should be making better use of our time than just sitting here."

"What did you have in mind?" she asked innocently.

He raised one eyebrow predatorily, then swept her off her feet and carried her into the bedroom. His lips stilled any further words she might have uttered. He pushed aside the offending gown and grazed his fingers over the silken skin of her stomach.

"If you only knew how many times I've touched you like this in my mind." His lips seared across hers again, then descended to the base of her neck.

Adrienne could feel herself slipping into a realm of sensations that seemed almost too blissful to be real. But some things felt very real, like the smooth expanse of his back that her fingers glided over. And the black froth of his hair that teased against the skin at the base of her neck while his lips branded kisses in the valley where her breasts met. His hands caressed and cajoled until her whole body flowered to life.

This time when they became one she felt more than the

143

wonder of their physical union. She felt as if he belonged completely to her, and she to him. The passion between them began as a gentle, swaying rhythm, with her body curving into response to his every nuance and fevered touch. Gradually, irrevocably, the waltz became more frenzied and erotic, and her body was a willing captive of his, depending on him for the fulfillment she sensed was just beyond her grasp.

And then he pressed her closer to him, and everything was within her grasp, and her head wheeled with the dizzying, voluptuous sensation of rapture.

It was several moments before the afterglow that flushed her body died away and her breathing became regular enough so that she could speak.

He sucked in a deep breath. "This wasn't what I had in mind when I came to your house yesterday, but I'm glad it happened."

She fitted herself into the crook of his arm and smiled as she felt his hand skimming over the curve of her hips. "What did you have in mind?" she asked teasingly.

He shrugged, a limber movement of his shoulders that she felt against her own body. "I don't know. I guess I just wanted to be with you. I didn't think much beyond that."

"I'm glad you came back here with me last night. I probably would have got depressed in the house by myself."

"Why?"

"I had a rather upsetting experience on Saturday."

144

Adrienne found herself telling him about Malcolm, the horse, even the need to raise money for Hopewell.

Christopher heard her out in silence.

"Got any suggestions?" she finally asked.

"Every kid knows what it's like to pine for something," he said slowly. "If Malcolm were any other kid, I'd say he was just going to have to learn to live without some things. But this isn't just any case. Malcolm's already alone in the world. It'd be a damn shame if he couldn't have the horse."

Propping herself up on one elbow, she watched the way the thick dark lashes slanted closer together as his eyes narrowed and he lost himself in thought.

She waited to hear what he would say. But when Christopher finally spoke again, it was about Hopewell—not Malcolm. "Maybe the best way to raise money for the place is to do short commercials using the boys themselves. It wouldn't have to be anything fancy. They could just say this is their home and they need contributions to keep it open."

She knew immediately it was the perfect solution. Not only would it require little initial outlay, but she liked the fact that the boys would be speaking for themselves. "That's an excellent idea, Christopher. You really are smart."

"Of course," he said without a trace of modesty. "I thought you already knew that."

"And modest," she added as she reached for the ticklish area of his ribs.

145

He wrestled her back into submission, kissed the tip of her nose, and lay back down beside her.

Although Christopher had to leave on Monday afternoon, Adrienne floated through the rest of the day. She was as distracted as she could ever remember being. She couldn't concentrate on anything without stopping to stare into the distance and thinking about something he had said or the way he had touched her.

But as she dressed for work on Tuesday morning in a pale green suit, Adrienne had a dim sense of foreboding. She resolutely thrust it aside in favor of the glorious memory of Sunday night, and she breezed into the office, distributing joyful smiles to one and all.

Her smile dimmed when she stepped into her office and found Mark waiting there. He didn't waste time trying to soften the blow. "Big problems, Adrienne. A couple of our biggest accounts are cutting time with us."

She looked at him sharply. "Who?"

"Hudson and Rowland. They're going to split their account between us and KTOO."

The joy drained out of her, and she raised her hand in a feeble gesture. "Why? Did you ask them?"

"Of course I asked! They've been lured away because KTOO has hired a classy ad agency out of Chicago to work on glitzy new commercials."

Gregg, who had followed Adrienne in, stood lounging near the door, listening impassively. "Want to hear the bad news now?" he asked with a weak attempt at humor.

Her chest constricted. "I'd hoped that *was* the bad news."

"Nope. Read this." He walked to her desk and pitched a manila folder across it.

Adrienne picked it up with a mounting sense of doom. "Something tells me I'm going to regret looking at this," she said. She was right. While it was only a preliminary survey, it showed that KXMZ had lost a substantial number of listeners over the previous month. It didn't take much insight to figure out who had picked up those listeners.

"We-l-l-l-l." She expelled the word as one long sigh, then forced herself to go on. "I guess we're going to have to get a lot more aggressive to keep our listeners tuned in to us. Gregg, why don't you check with Ralph and find out if he has anything in the planning stages for station promotion?" She glanced at her calendar. "I'm busy this afternoon, but tomorrow morning, first thing, I want to get everything together and brainstorm for some good suggestions to increase our ratings." She jotted notes to herself as she spoke.

To anyone looking at her she thought she presented a cool and collected picture. No one had any way of knowing that it felt as if someone were twisting her insides.

Mark nodded his approval. "Good idea."

Gregg ran his fingers over the top of his head where the hair had receded. "I sure never thought poor old KTOO would pull itself up by its outdated bootstraps the way it has. Kind of makes me respect the people there in spite of myself."

Adrienne stretched her mouth into a grim smile. "I know what you mean."

"Too bad Christopher Ames is so likable," Gregg continued. "Of course, he's offering some good amenities to his advertisers, but I think he's winning some of them on charm alone."

"Yes, I believe he is," she said tonelessly, battling to hold back the irrational resentment that surged through her. *He had no right to do this to her!* If he was going to offer her business competition, the least he could have done was have the courtesy to be humpbacked and crosseyed. But no, he had swung into her life looking boldly handsome and brimming with charm. Worse, he was capable of singeing her with smoldering kisses that could undermine her best defenses. And why was she thinking about those kisses at the worst possible moment—like now—when she should be concentrating on solving the problems Christopher was creating?

"I've got to run," Mark called from the doorway. "I have an appointment. I'll see you later."

"I have to go, too," Gregg joined in.

She looked up listlessly. "Bye."

As soon as the door closed behind them, Adrienne's tightly controlled anger began to sizzle. She was angry with Christopher and angry with herself, and logic wasn't particularly important at the moment. Just when she had begun to trust him, *this* happened. He had no right to do this to her! And how could she possibly handle a personal relationship while they were caught in a tense professional rivalry?

She couldn't, she resolved as her anger crystallized into determination. Maybe it wasn't fair to blame Christopher. Maybe this bad situation was no one's fault. But the fact was that circumstances were bigger than both of them. And that left their romance in the middle to be crushed by the weight of other responsibilities.

Sighing, she slumped farther back in her chair. She didn't regret Sunday night. Or Monday morning. Being with Christopher had been the most important thing in the world to her then. But it had to end.

Christopher glanced back at the latest ratings survey that lay on his desk and suffered again an uncomfortable premonition of how this was going to affect his relationship with Adrienne. KTOO had gained considerably while KXMZ had lost some of its share of the audience. The result was that the two were now vying for the top position. She was dedicated to her job, he knew; she was going to take this hard.

It was almost eight o'clock in the evening, but he was still at the office. After picking up the phone, he dialed Adrienne's home number. When no one answered, he dialed her work number.

She answered it on the second ring. "KXMZ. Adrienne Donnelly." Her voice sounded thin and cheerless.

"It's Christopher."

"Oh . . . hello."

The chilly silence that followed said more than words ever could. Brusquely he pushed his fingers through his hair and forged on. "How would you like to meet me for a drink?"

"I don't think so, Christopher."

Over the past two months he'd grown used to hearing her turn him down, but he'd never heard such finality in her words before.

"The truth is I don't think we should see each other anymore," she continued. "I know I've said that before," she added with a mirthless laugh, "but believe me, this time I mean it. I'm sorry things didn't work out," she said impassively.

"Don't do this, Adrienne." He broke in harshly. "I know you're upset about the ratings. But we can at least get together and talk."

"What's the point?" she asked tiredly.

His fist curled more tightly around the receiver, and his mouth pinched into a narrow line. "The point is that we can work out any problems between us." Didn't she understand that? Defeat was only for those who accepted it. He'd learned that when he'd lost his money in the oil deal and had wallowed in his misery instead of trying to solve his problems.

Adrienne laughed brittlely. "You make it sound so simple, but I'm afraid it isn't."

"It *is* if you want it to be. Oh, I'm not blind or stubborn enough to deny there's bound to be some friction between us because of our work, but anything can be negotiated if both people want to."

"I'm sorry, but I don't happen to think so. Good-bye."

That was all. Seconds later Christopher found himself

listening to a dial tone. He sighed heavily. So it had finally come to this. Adrienne had evaded and avoided him from the very beginning because of the "competition" inherent in their jobs. It had been an excuse then because she hadn't wanted to get involved. As far as he was concerned, it was still an excuse, but now she *was* involved with him. Why was she fighting that so hard?

## CHAPTER TEN

The next day, when Adrienne met with Boswell at his office, she told him about the idea about having the boys themselves raise money by appearing on television and radio. Boswell was impressed with the straightforward concept. Adrienne didn't tell him it hadn't been her idea.

"We don't want the kids to beg," she noted. "We'll just have them tell in their own words that Hopewell is where they live and that money is needed to keep it open."

"We won't even have an initial outlay of money the way we might have if we'd adopted some other money-making projects."

"No, we won't," she said. She ought to feel a lot more enthusiastic about the project than she did. But all that she'd been able to feel since talking to Christopher yesterday was a dull, gnawing ache that had pursued her even when she was asleep. Consequently, she had awakened this morning feeling tired and anxious.

"I'll tell you what," Boswell continued eagerly. "I'll talk to the television station managers and arrange for public service time, and you talk to the radio station managers."

She shook her head. "I'd—I'd rather talk to the TV people." He looked at her curiously but agreed. Because she couldn't explain to him that she didn't want to have to see Christopher, she just let Boswell believe she was being temperamental.

Adrienne had reviewed yesterday's telephone conversation with Christopher over and over in her mind, playing it back like a record she couldn't get enough of. He had seemed so confident they could work things out. If only that were true! But their stations were ranged against each other like two armies preparing to do battle. They had reached an impasse . . . hadn't they?

But the certainty she had felt yesterday had been diluted by a fitful night of sleep and the anguish of their parting. Did her real fear of Christopher even have anything to do with the station or was she afraid of something far less definable?

Boswell broke into her thoughts. "Do you think we should have several different kids doing the commercials or just one?"

"Uh, I think it might be nice to have more than one."

She forced her attention back to the present, and they settled down to discuss the particulars.

A week passed. The blustery November wind grew colder as fall edged into winter. Adrienne attacked her work as if there would be no tomorrow. At home she tried to do the same. She packed away her fall clothes and got out winter wools. She rearranged the living room furniture. She bought a wok and experimented with Chinese cooking. But there was a lonely edge to everything she did, and her apartment had never seemed so sterile and empty.

*I'll get over him,* she had told herself a hundred times. It was one of the things she repeated to herself when she awoke in the middle of the night feeling desolate.

Plans for the fund-raising commercials were in full swing, and she spent some time almost every day at Hopewell, helping pick out locations for the filming, talking to the boys, and conferring with Boswell.

During her frequent trips there she often saw Malcolm, and it pulled at her heartstrings when she did. He had returned to being a quiet, serious boy. The flash of excitement and eagerness she had witnessed when he showed her his good grades had been buried again. He still wanted the horse, she was sure, and she promised herself she would work on that—after the public service messages had been taken care of.

And of course, she had known it was inevitable she would see Christopher again. But she hadn't expected to see him at Hopewell. On the Saturday before Thanksgiving, however, they came face-to-face just inside the door of the home.

Rattled by the unexpectedness of the meeting, Adrienne was at a total loss for words. She merely stared at him.

"Hello, Adrienne," he said formally.

She remained rooted to the spot, drinking him in with

her eyes. Over the past three weeks she had almost convinced herself she had exaggerated how handsome he was. But seeing him reaffirmed his male beauty. His mouth was the perfect shape of an archer's bow, and his blue-gray eyes were awarded even more prominence by the edging of black lashes. His jaw was definite without being aggressive. His hair looked well cut but natural, showing that he was a man who cared about his appearance but didn't fuss over it. She felt an ache of longing that threatened to buckle her knees.

"Can't you even speak to me, Adrienne?"

"I'm sorry," she managed to say in a shallow voice that didn't sound like her own. "I'm just surprised to see you here, that's all."

"I came to see the boys."

Again she didn't know what to say. She couldn't fathom his mood or his feelings beneath his polite façade. Did he feel the same jolt of longing as she? Or did he feel anything at all for her any longer?

"In fact," he continued with a trace of a smile, "I've brought something for them that I'd like you to see, too. It's out back." When she continued to stand wordlessly, he took her arm. "I'll show you." She fell mechanically into step beside him, and they started down the long hall toward the back door.

As they walked, Adrienne breathed in the subtle scent of his masculine aftershave until she felt she would drown in it. She couldn't think clearly while he was so close to her. But, oh, how good it felt to be this close to him again.

He pushed open the back door, and they stepped out into the wind. "Over there," he said, pointing toward a small fenced-in area near the ball field. Boys were lined all around the perimeter of the fence, while inside a dozen colts danced and bucked.

She stopped, staring at the colts. The sight of them brought her out of her trance. "Where did they come from?"

"I bought them," he said simply.

Astonished, she turned to him. "You bought them. But they must have cost you a fortune!"

He shook his head calmly. "No. They're wild mustangs, and they would have been destroyed if someone hadn't bought them."

"Wild mustangs," she repeated dumbly, "but these are young boys. They can't handle wild animals."

"I've talked to the owner of a stable near here. He's agreed to break them in for us. It's tax-deductible," he added, and this time his smile touched into his eyes.

She felt self-conscious, almost shy, as his eyes played over her face. "It—it's very nice of you, Christopher." He was a nice man—kind and thoughtful—the kind of man most women searched for all their lives and never found. Was she making a devastating mistake not to hold on to him in the face of all odds?

"Come on," he said with sudden enthusiasm, "let's go take a closer look."

Again he took her arm, and they hurried down the steps and across the baseball field to the fenced-in area. The gleeful shouts of the boys were carried away on the wind, but she could see the delight shining in each face. Especially Malcolm's.

"Christopher." She pulled him to a stop, and he turned to her questioningly. "Thank you," she said warmly. "Thank you very much." She was thanking him for more than the horses, and she knew he understood that. She was thanking him for realizing how important it was to Malcolm and thanking him for being sensitive enough to go to all this trouble partly on her behalf. She got a warm feeling knowing he'd taken her worries so much to heart that he'd done something to ease them.

He nodded, looking at her intently.

They continued over to the fence in silence, but it was a different, more agreeable silence from what she had felt only minutes before. Adrienne stopped at the wooden railing beside Malcolm and tousled his hair companionably.

She smiled at the boy. "What do you think of them?"

"I love them! The palomino's mine. And Kenny's," he added after a moment's hesitation.

"You don't mind sharing, do you?" Adrienne asked carefully.

"No, not as long as it's just with one other person. And not as long as I know I can be with him on Saturday mornings."

"Saturday morning?"

"Yes, I'm going to clean out the stables to earn his room and board. So are the other boys."

"I see."

"Nothing should be given to you outright," Malcolm

told her seriously and turned back to watch the horses cavorting in the field.

"No, of course not," she murmured. Adrienne had a sneaking suspicion Malcolm was repeating Christopher's words.

"Nice-looking animals, aren't they?" Christopher said conversationally from her other side.

Infected by Malcolm's contagious happiness, she smiled at Christopher. "They're beautiful. It was a wonderful idea to buy wild mustangs." With blunt candor she continued. "So tell me, how did you come up with such an easy solution to a problem I've worried over for weeks?"

"Maybe I just tried harder." A wealth of meaning glimmered in his smoky blue eyes.

She turned back to look at the horses. "Maybe you did," she said lightly. But she knew he was really saying if she had tried as hard as he to make things work between them, they could have had something together.

Malcolm looked up at her. "I'm going to name my horse Pilgrim 'cause I got him close to Thanksgiving."

"That's a nice name," she said. She stroked Malcolm's hair down and added, "You *are* going to keep your grades up now that you have a horse, aren't you?"

He nodded solemnly. "Yes, ma'am. I promised Christopher I would. We had a man-to-man talk about it."

Adrienne was torn between a sigh and a smile. Once again Christopher was succeeding where she had failed.

Malcolm's eyes had wandered lovingly back out to the

field of horses. "Don't you think Pilgrim is a good name?"

She nodded. "Very nice."

"I'm gonna go home for Thanksgiving." He lowered his voice and leaned closer. "Some of the boys don't get to. They're goin' home with Mr. Simmons or one of the other houseparents. I felt kinda sorry for them, but then Christopher said he didn't have anywhere to go Thanksgiving either and no one to be with, so then I didn't feel so bad about those kids that have to go home with houseparents."

Guilt stabbed at her. Christopher had gone to a good deal of trouble to get these horses for the boys. Yet what was anyone doing for him? She was going to her parents for the holiday. Didn't she owe it to him to invite him along for a home-cooked meal? Maybe the first he'd had on Thanksgiving in years? But inviting him might imply that she wanted to push beyond the boundaries of friendship again.

Christopher pushed himself away from the fence. "I guess I'd better be going. It was nice seeing you, Adrienne," he said without inflection.

*He was going to spend Thanksgiving alone if she didn't say something.* Still, she stood rooted to the spot.

"Thanks for the horse!" Malcolm shouted, and a dozen other boys added their voices.

Christopher was halfway back to the building before Adrienne made up her mind. "Wait!" she called and ran to catch up with him. When she did, she gasped out

159

breathlessly, "Thanksgiving's this week. Do you have any plans?"

He watched her curiously. "No."

"Why don't you come home with me? To my parents' house." She paused to take several deep breaths. "I'll be driving down there the night before and coming back the day after."

He looked at her intently. "Are you sure?"

She grinned with sudden mischief. "Well, no, I could come back the same day or I could wait until two days after Thanksgiving before coming back or I could—"

"Adrienne," he said with smooth menace, "you're going to get yourself thrown into the field with those wild horses."

She tossed her head defiantly. "You do, and I'll see to it that you don't get a drumstick at Thanksgiving."

"Are you sure your parents won't mind an unexpected guest?" he asked.

But she knew the question was just for the sake of politeness. Christopher had already made up his mind to go. "They'll be glad to have you," she assured him. And she would, too. She didn't like to think of his spending the holiday alone or eating at a restaurant. Thanksgiving should be warm and special, and she wanted to make it that way for him, especially after what he had done for the boys.

"I'll see you Wednesday night," he said.

"I can certainly understand what you see in him," Adrienne's mother, Catherine, leaned over to confide as they poured drinks in the kitchen. "He's a very charming young man."

"We're just friends, Mom." It had to have been the dozenth time Adrienne had tried to get that point across to her mother.

"Of course, dear." Her mother patted her on the shoulder with patent disbelief.

*They're still hoping I'll fall in love again,* Adrienne thought as she carried drinks into the paneled den and handed one to Christopher. Both her parents had expressed great interest in the men in her life ever since she'd begun dating again after Bobby's death. They never actually pushed her, but she knew they wanted to see her happy, and for them, that involved a house and children. Their own marriage had been blissful, so Adrienne supposed it was natural they would want the same for her.

"I was just telling Christopher about the college," her father, James Donnelly, said.

Catherine settled into a wing chair. "Yes, we're very proud of our little college here in Lebanon."

Adrienne sat down on the edge of her father's chair and leaned against him as he talked about McKendree College, the oldest Methodist college in the Middle West. She watched with affection as he spoke. Her father had suffered a mild heart attack last year, and the lines in his face were deeper now. But he still held himself erect, and he still had a full, if graying, head of hair.

Adrienne's glance flowed to her mother. Catherine's hair was still brown, but Adrienne knew it was with the help of a bottle. And there were age lines in her face, too, although they accented, rather than diminished, the daintiness of her features. When she smiled, the wrinkles seemed to vanish, and Adrienne could see again the younger woman she had known as a child.

Adrienne's gaze drifted to Christopher. He was listening to her father with an expression of schooled interest, but she saw him look now and again toward the wedding picture of her and Bobby on the mantel. She had never told Christopher about her marriage, she realized, as he batted another, seemingly casual, look toward the mantel.

". . . called McKendree College now," James was saying, "but it was founded in 1828 as Lebanon Seminary by pioneers. Very pretty campus. It sits on the highest part of town and—"

"James," Adrienne's mother interrupted, "don't you think it's time you and I took Gunner out for a walk?"

"Heh?"

"Don't you think we should take the dog for a walk, dear? And while we're out, I want to stop in at the Joneses'." She smiled first at Adrienne, then at Christopher. "We'll be back in a couple of hours. I'm sure the young people won't object. Adrienne can show Christopher where everything is around the house, or they can watch television or play cards or something. . . ." Her words dwindled off vaguely, but the glimmer in her eye seemed to say, *I was young once, and I understand that young people want to be alone.*

"It's kind of chilly out," James said testily.

"Nonsense. It's merely brisk. I'll get your coat." Catherine left and returned a few minutes later with two coats.

"I still think it's awful cold to be out," Adrienne's father muttered.

"Come along, dear," her mother said sweetly.

A moment later Adrienne heard the back door close followed by Gunner's excited barks. A smile rose unbidden to her lips.

Christopher's smile matched her own. "I think your mother was trying to give us a little time alone. I'm not so sure your father understood that."

Adrienne nodded, laughing now. "Poor Mom, she's been trying for years to instill some tact in Dad, but she hasn't had much luck. I love him dearly, but he can be a bore at times. Mother's had to save someone from his clutches at every cocktail party they've ever been to."

Her smile flickered as she became aware Christopher was watching her with steady purpose. He was dressed in a navy cashmere pullover and houndstooth check slacks. It was impossible not to notice how the fine worsted wool of his slacks revealed the hard lines of the leg muscles beneath.

He looked back toward the wedding picture. "I didn't know you'd ever been married."

Adrienne slid off the arm of the chair. "It was a long time ago. He died. Would you like to see the rest of the house?" she asked.

Christopher didn't budge. "No. Do you still love him?"

163

"Of course not. I told you, he's dead. Why don't we watch television?"

He rose with slow precision and fitted his hands into his pockets. "Why did you invite me here?" he asked quietly.

"Because . . . well, because I didn't think you'd have any other plans for Thanksgiving." She bit her lip. "No, that's not true. Not really." Lifting her head, she looked into his tense, waiting face. "I invited you because I've been lonely and miserable without you and I thought—I thought—" She shrugged helplessly. "I don't know what I thought."

He took his hands out of his pockets, crossed over to her, and slid them around her waist. "I think we're finally getting somewhere."

She blinked up at him. "We are?"

He chuckled softly, as if to himself. "Yes, we are." His lips brushed across hers while his hands moved to her hips, and he pulled her closer against him.

She wanted him, she realized with a blinding flash of longing. And there was no way to misjudge the somnolent, sensual look in his eyes. He wanted her, too, and that emboldened her.

"Come on," she whispered, taking his hand as she began to lead him out of the room. He followed obediently up the stairs and into her frilly pink bedroom, looking around briefly before she flipped out the light.

"This room has been the scene of a lot of fantasies but no real exploits," she confided in a whisper. They were alone in the house, but somehow it seemed like a sacrilege to talk to a man in her girlhood bedroom.

He laughed huskily. "Why don't we see about changing that?"

"Yes, why don't we?" she answered and forgot to whisper. As she went into his arms again, she sensed that a lot of things had changed and were still changing between them. She felt no reserve with him, and for the first time in as long as she could remember she wanted to let herself go, flying without a net and experiencing not only the physical but the full extent of the emotional rewards of being part of another person.

They tumbled onto the bed together, she on top. Adrienne sensed his surprise as she tugged his sweater off him with unabashed zeal. Once the sweater had been discarded, she caressed his chest, letting her palms glide over the few wiry hairs and circling the taut, flat nipples. She dipped her head for a brief, fiery kiss, then started to move away again. But Christopher wouldn't allow that. His lips quickened on hers, and he locked her in the velvet prison of his embrace.

A moment later she found herself beneath him, and it was his hands that were creating swirls and currents of pure pleasure on her stomach and thighs. He made short work of the buttons on her blouse, pushing aside the soft cotton shirt as if it were as coarse and offending as horsehair. Then he was branding kisses on her shoulders, her neck, her breasts.

She sighed and wriggled contentedly.

He sighed, too, but sharply. "If you do that again, this is going to be over a lot sooner than you think."

"Do what?"

"Move your hips like that."

"Like this?" she asked innocently and demonstrated.

He swore and rolled to the edge of the bed. She heard the remainder of his clothes hit the floor. Then he pulled hers off and reclaimed her with a burning kiss. His hands explored with bold familiarity that still contained a sensuous understanding of a woman's needs. He knew where to touch her to make her catch her breath, and he knew how to massage her to make her whimper with helpless longing.

But she was his equal in bestowing pleasure. Her own hands aroused and caressed and tantalized until his breathing was a ragged edge. With slipping control he lifted her to him and pressed himself into her.

At first they moved together slowly. She grazed her fingers over the corded strength of his back as his kisses became more forceful and urgent while his hand toyed with the floret of her nipple. She wanted this feeling of bliss to go on and on even as she yearned for the even greater sensations that she knew would eventually sweep down on them.

His body was fully in control now, and he increased the pace of their movements with steady, sure intent. Adrienne was caught in the spell of the witchery of eroticism. Every movement he made translated itself to her body and vibrated through her.

And then she lost track of all rational thought and

gave herself over to the arc of bright colors and the shiver of exquisite satisfaction that invaded her to her very being.

As her erratic breathing measured the irregularity of her heartbeat, he scooped her closer into his arms and held her against him. "How does reality compare to the fantasies?" he asked hoarsely.

"Better," she murmured with smug contentment. "Much better."

## CHAPTER ELEVEN

"We bought the house in '45," James explained to Christopher as they sat at the kitchen table over their morning coffee. It was still early, and they were the first two up. "No—no, wait, I believe it was '46. Anyway, it was right after the war. Barbara, that's our older girl—the one who lives in Boston—was born right away. We wanted a playmate for her as soon as possible, but Sissy took her own sweet time. She wasn't born until Barbara was eight."

Christopher looked at him over the rim of his cup. "Sissy? Is that what you call Adrienne?"

"That's what everybody called her until she was thirteen or so. Then she decided it wasn't sophisticated enough." James chuckled reflectively. "Oh, my, you can't imagine how sophisticated and worldly-wise our Adrienne was at thirteen."

Christopher laughed. "I'll bet." He could imagine what she must have looked like then with the brown eyes not yet seductive but wanting to be. And at that age she had probably construed the red in her glorious hair as a curse.

"That was right about the time she discovered *boys,*" her father confided.

"Made a big impression on her, did they?" Christopher was thoroughly enjoying this glimpse into Adrienne's past.

"I should say they did! All of a sudden it took her half an hour to comb her hair and a good hour to pick out what she was going to wear to school. Those were *all* major decisions, mind you. Sometimes she had to call in reinforcements to help make up her mind, and we'd have a whole bunch of giggling girls cluttering up the house." Smiling reflectively, he rose. "How about some more coffee?"

"No, thanks."

"Ah, yes, seems like it was only yesterday when she started having boys calling at the house."

Christopher's expression grew speculative. There was one boy in particular from Adrienne's past Christopher wanted to learn more about. "How old was Adrienne when she got married?"

"Seventeen." James returned to his chair with a full cup of coffee. "Bobby was eighteen. I know it seems young, but Catherine and I were that age when we got married. Besides, how can you refuse to give your permission to two kids who're in love?" His lips firmed into a dry smile. "Between you and me, *I* probably could have refused, but Catherine wouldn't hear of it. Of course, the way things turned out Adrienne might have been better off if we'd insisted that she wait."

169

Christopher tilted his head curiously. "The way things turned out?"

"Well, yeah," James said stoutly, as if repeating a fact known universally, "he may have been a good-looking so-and-so, and he had enough charm to dazzle the ladies, but I think he was running around on Sissy within two years of their wedding."

James paused, and Christopher stirred some more sugar into his coffee and looked around the cheerful kitchen casually. He was anxious to hear more about Adrienne's marriage.

"Anyway, Bobby got killed in a fire at the plant where he worked, and Sissy was pretty broken up over it, but eventually she went back to school."

"Did she—"

"Well, good morning! You two are up early." Catherine paused to brush a kiss across her husband's cheek. "Goodness, you've even made the coffee. I'll just have a cup of that, and then I've got to get the turkey started."

Adrienne didn't get up for another hour. When she finally strolled into the den, she looked well rested and cuddly in an oversize flannel shirt and tousled hair. Christopher had to satisfy himself with merely smiling at her.

"After dinner I'll show you the town," she promised him before heading off to the kitchen with the announcement "I'm starving, Mom. What's for breakfast?"

Adrienne had always been proud of her hometown, but she hadn't looked at the quaint Victorian brick buildings downtown or the pretty rolling campus of McKendree College with such appreciation for a long time. Perhaps she was enjoying the scenery so much because Christopher was such an enthusiastic sightseer.

"Very pleasant rural sort of town," he said as they walked hand in hand through the city park. The fallen leaves that formed a blanket on the ground here and there had been raked into thick piles.

"Yes," she murmured contentedly. "It's a nice change from the fast pace of the city, yet it's so close to St. Louis —only thirty miles—that people can pop over there anytime they like to go shopping or out to a nice dinner."

The crisp leaves beneath their feet rustled noisily as they walked. Nearby a squirrel darted toward a tree with a nut in hand. Farther away children frolicked on slides and swings.

"Your father tells me you used to be called Sissy," Christopher said, nudging his shoulder against hers and laughing down at her.

She put the weight of her shoulder against his and pushed back. "That's not fair. I don't have anyone to talk to to find out dirt about you."

He stepped deftly away from her, removing her support so that she began to fall. "Christopher!"

He caught her up by the waist, lifted her off her feet, and carried her to a nearby pile of leaves. "So you want dirt on me, do you, Sissy? All right, I'll tell you—I used to lie and tell my mother I'd washed behind my ears when I hadn't." She was laughing as he dropped her onto the thick cushion of leaves and swooped down after her.

171

*"And* I once cheated on a third-grade math test. Shocking stuff, huh? Too bad you won't live to tell my dark secrets to anyone. I'm going to bury you right here in these leaves," he announced and began tossing fistfuls of leaves over her.

Still laughing, Adrienne tried to get up, but he pushed her back down. *Oh, well,* she decided cheerfully, *all's fair in love and war.* She'd simply lure him into the leaves and then cover *him.* As he scattered more handfuls of leaves over her, she reached up and caught her hands behind his neck, lowering her lashes and pouting seductively.

He paused. The playful fire in his eyes quickly became something much more masculine. And definitely intrigued.

Now that she had him on the line, there was only one way to reel him in. She raised her head and skimmed her lips across his, then settled in for a more leisurely examination. After only the slightest hesitation he covered her body with his and brushed his knuckles across her cheek. The leaves whispered against her ears as she sank deeper into the cave they made. He drew her so tightly against him that thigh touched thigh and her breasts were pressed against the hardness of his chest.

Her purpose in enticing him into this kiss was momentarily forgotten as she gave herself over to the persuasive pressure of his mouth. And a moment later her lips yielded to the delicious entreaty of his tongue. The soft moan of pleasure that rippled up from her throat was lost in the chattering of the surrounding leaves. She wished they were back in the privacy of her bedroom so that they could complete what was starting so wonderfully.

Christopher must have been thinking the same thing. For he drew away from her, sighed regretfully, then pulled himself to his feet. A mischievous smile spread over his face as he surveyed her. She was sunk deep in a cocoon of leaves now, and he began completing the cover by adding more leaves atop her.

Still feeling the ebbing pleasure of his kisses, she lay in passive contentment. What he could do to her with just a few kisses, she thought happily, and filled her eyes with the sight of him standing there in the sun: a beautiful, broad-shouldered, long-legged celebration of the flesh. Then he dusted a few leaves over her face, and she lost sight of him.

Above her Christopher cleared his throat formally. "I'd like to say a few words over the dearly departed—Sissy."

"Adrienne," she said in correction.

"Quiet. It's in poor taste for a corpse to speak at her own funeral."

She giggled and stuck her foot out.

"I wouldn't do that if I were you. There's a dog coming."

That did it. Adrienne pushed back her covering and jumped up. Of course, there was no dog—only Christopher watching her with a grin. In his eyes, though, she could see a last flicker of unquenched desire. Oh, how she wished she could satisfy that desire, and her own in the bargain. But circumstances being what they were, she

173

had to content herself with whispering a provocative promise into his ear.

Later that afternoon Christopher stood in the Donnellys' big backyard and watched as Adrienne threw a stick and urged Gunner to retrieve it.

"Come on, boy. Fetch! You remember how to fetch," she coaxed. "Sure you do, boy."

He stifled his laughter. Gunner, a reddish collie that looked as if he had been on the wrong end of more than one fight, merely looked curiously from Adrienne to the stick, clearly confused about what was expected of him.

She picked up the stick and tried again. "Fetch, Gunner. Show Christopher what you can do, ol' boy."

"He's really a very bright dog," Catherine assured Christopher from his left side.

On his right side Adrienne's father snorted. "Dumbest mutt I've ever seen in my life. I don't know why we've kept him."

"Hush," his wife admonished, then glanced at her watch. "Uh-oh! I'd better go check on the turkey. I'm only rewarming it, so I don't want to leave it in too long. James, why don't you come help me?"

"I don't know anything about turkeys," he grumbled, but he went anyway.

Christopher watched them leave, then strolled over to where Adrienne stood in the large sloping yard. "Now *I* used to have a dog that understood the meaning of the word 'fetch.' A beagle. It was a present from my father.

174

At my mother's instigation," he added with a reminiscent laugh.

Adrienne patted Gunner before linking her arm through Christopher's. "Well, Gunner may have forgotten how to fetch, but he's a very good guard dog."

"I'm sure he is," he said, but he wasn't particularly interested in dogs anyway. His eyes kept straying to her. Adrienne looked especially pretty today with the fresh air bringing a natural glow to her cheeks and the gold in her hair catching in the fall sunlight. And her oversize flannel shirt and faded jeans curiously emphasized the supple litheness of her figure.

He was glad he had come home with her for Thanksgiving. The trip had provided insight into Adrienne that he didn't think he ever would have gotten in St. Louis. Learning that she had been married and that her husband had betrayed her gave him new understanding of why she was so afraid to give her heart to a man. It also explained why she had been dating Ned and probably a whole raft of other men before that who wouldn't demand any intense emotional or sexual ties. Even as far as he and Adrienne were concerned, he could see that it had been convenient for her that they were in professional competition; it offered an excuse for her not to get close to him.

"Christopher . . ." she began.

He glanced up at her as she hesitated and ran her hand across her upper lip. "Yes?"

"About last night . . ."

He waited for her to continue.

"I—I like you a great deal. I don't want to lose you,

175

but I don't know how things will turn out once we're back in St. Louis. I'm a very competitive person," she added with a weak, apologetic smile. "I don't mean to let things come between us, but they—they might." She didn't say so, but there was something more than that. Even while she was happy with Christopher, she was reluctant to commit herself too far.

He looked away from her and squinted thoughtfully up at the sky. Last night Adrienne had told him, in deeds, if not in words, that she loved him. But somehow she still wasn't able to admit that to herself. Was that why she wanted to leave herself an escape hatch? Only he wasn't going to let her, he resolved before turning to her with an indecipherable smile.

"We probably should go in and help set the table, don't you think?" he suggested.

Adrienne looked at him quizzically, then nodded. "Yes, I suppose so."

"He's real smart," Malcolm told Adrienne on Sunday as the boy stood watching the strutting palomino with undisguised adoration. "He knows his name when I call him."

She nodded and smiled absently. The day before, she and Christopher had driven back from her parents' house, and she had been expecting him to spend the night with her. In fact, she had been counting on it. But he had seemed preoccupied during the drive back, and when they'd pulled up in front of her house and she'd invited him in, he'd declined.

Probably he had just been tired, she told herself. Or perhaps he, like she, had had a great deal to think about. During the time they'd spent together in Lebanon, she'd felt her perceptions about him and about herself changing.

Malcolm tugged at her arm. "Pilgrim's the prettiest horse out there, don't you think?"

"What? The prettiest? Yes, definitely," she said and smiled in what she hoped was Pilgrim's direction. Although she wouldn't have told Malcolm so for the world, Adrienne had a hard time telling Pilgrim from the two other palominos.

"Mr. Simmons says they've started breaking the horses. I hope Pilgrim's ready to ride soon," Malcolm said wistfully.

"I'm sure he will be," she murmured and allowed Malcolm to gaze at the colt for a few moments longer before saying, "We'd better be getting back to the home."

He cast a yearning look at Pilgrim, then turned and followed her to her car.

"Are you studying hard?" she asked as she eased the car down the rutted driveway toward the highway.

"Yes, ma'am." Malcolm twisted in the seat for a final look at the horse.

Adrienne couldn't help smiling. The animated boy in the seat beside her seemed a far cry from the listless Malcolm she had first known. All he had needed was something special and important in his life, and Christopher had supplied that when he'd given him the horse. Now Malcolm was motivated.

Her smile softened to a thoughtful expression. Christopher had given her new motivation as well. Before he had arrived, she had been complacent at the station. Oh, she'd done a good job, but since Christopher had begun making changes at KTOO, she had begun demanding a great deal more of herself. She'd had to in order to compete with Christopher.

And he had changed her personal life as well, she acknowledged. Before she met him, she had contentedly settled for a passionless relationship. Now she wanted more. Now—

Malcolm tapped her arm. "You missed the turnoff to Hopewell."

She switched her attention back to the road. "I guess I wasn't watching what I was doing. Sorry."

"That's 'kay," Malcolm said magnanimously.

She turned around at the next road and this time took the right route to the home, deliberately keeping her thoughts from drifting to Christopher.

When they arrived at Hopewell, Malcolm went upstairs to finish some homework while Adrienne stopped at Mr. Simmons's office. "Are you ready for the big day of filming tomorrow?" she asked cheerfully.

He grinned at her. "Everybody here is raring to go."

All the boys had written essays on what living at Hopewell meant to them, and five had been selected to speak in front of the camera.

"I think we're really going to get a good response from the audience," she told him. Almost every radio and television station in the area had donated public service time for the messages.

"I think so, too," he agreed.

They talked for several more minutes before she left. Adrienne spent the rest of the evening in her apartment. At first she tried to lure herself into the plot of a best seller, but eventually she gave up on that and contented herself with puttering around and waiting for the phone to ring.

It didn't.

She and Christopher had had no quarrel, and just because he hadn't come in last night was no real cause for concern. Was it? Logically she could tell herself no. But a feeling of foreboding was growing within.

And still the phone didn't ring.

*Well, this is the eighties,* she told herself briskly. What was stopping her from calling Christopher? But something stayed her hand each time it reached for the phone. He had not come in last night for a nightcap. And he had not called her tonight. Were those simply two separate instances that meant nothing? Or did they mean something very significant?

Folding her hands across her chest, she paced to the sliding balcony door and looked out. Beneath the night lights she could see the leafless trees and a landscape that looked bleak and brown. "Just the way I'm beginning to feel," she said aloud.

She was just turning away from the window when she saw Kelly's car pull up. She could use some companionship right now. Pushing open the balcony door, she shouted, "Kelly! Come on over."

Kelly nodded and waved in reply.

A few seconds later the pretty brunette was at her door.

"What've you been up to?" Adrienne asked.

"Shopping." She slipped out of her coat. "If you're wondering if it's too late to beat the Christmas rush, I can tell you that it definitely is. I was nearly trampled by the mob at the fragrance counter at Stix's."

"Hmmm."

Kelly sat on the sofa. "So how was Thanksgiving with Christopher?"

"Wonderful." Without her intending it to, her gaze slid toward the phone. At least the day in the park, seeing her hometown, and watching Christopher had been wonderful for her. But had something happened to change his opinion of her?

Kelly watched her appraisingly. "If it was so wonderful, why do I get the feeling something's bothering you?"

"It's nothing really." Adrienne sat in the wicker rocker and curled her feet up under her. Under Kelly's waiting gaze, she continued. "It's just that he seemed a little remote when we got back here last night, and I haven't heard from him today. Of course, he could be busy," she added quickly.

"Call him."

"Yes, I suppose I should," Adrienne said without conviction. "Maybe I will later."

"Call him *now*." For emphasis Kelly picked up the phone and handed it to her.

Shrugging with more indifference than she felt, Adrienne dialed Christopher's number and counted the rings. She was just getting ready to hang up when he answered.

"Hello, Christopher! It's Adrienne." Why did her smile feel tight and her voice determinedly upbeat?

Across from her Kelly nodded approvingly.

"Hi!" he said.

She began to breathe more easily, relieved by how cheerful he sounded. Leaning back more comfortably in the chair, she continued. "I thought maybe we could have dinner together tomorrow."

"Tomorrow? Gee, I'd love to, but I can't. Thanks for asking, though."

"Well, maybe some other time then."

"Sure," he said gaily. "Some other time would probably be fine. It was great hearing from you. I gotta run now. Bye."

"Bye," she repeated dazedly.

Kelly took the phone from her slack fingers and hung it up. "Something tells me I shouldn't have butted in and made you call him."

Adrienne shook her head to clear it. "I don't understand. Things were going so well at my parents' house. Of course," she added softly, half to herself, "I did tell him I wasn't sure what would happen once we got back to St. Louis."

Both women were silent for several moments.

"Maybe he thought you were going to give him the

181

brush-off, so he decided to beat you to it," Kelly ventured the thought cautiously.

"No." Christopher wasn't like that. Something must be bothering him. Maybe things weren't going well at work. There must be some good explanation. He would call her tomorrow and explain, and everything would be fine. After all, he was the one who had said they could work out any problems between them if they only wanted to. Yes, they would work everything out. She would tell him that when he called tomorrow.

But Monday slid slowly, painfully into Thursday, and Christopher didn't call. She couldn't count the times she reached for the phone to call him, but she never did. It hurt to think that he might be brushing her off, but it was easier than knowing for *sure* that he was, which is what he might tell her if they talked.

# CHAPTER TWELVE

With Christmas only one week away, Christopher found himself listening to "White Christmas" on the radio as he looked out his apartment window at the snowflakes that were just beginning to fall. It was time, he thought, and felt the familiar twist in his midsection. What if all his careful planning hadn't been careful enough? What if he hadn't understood Adrienne as well as he thought? But the keystone of all the questions—and the one he tried to avoid examining—was what if she didn't love him enough.

Adrienne did love him; he was sure of that. But he wanted an unconditional, unreserved love, and he wasn't sure she was willing, even able, to surrender that to him. After five years of keeping all men at bay, maybe she had the system down to perfection.

His strategy over the past three weeks had been a gamble, and he only hoped it paid off. One way or the other he was going to know tomorrow because as soon as he returned from the job interview in Chicago, he was going to talk to her. He didn't know if the decision to stay away from Adrienne for the past long weeks had been wise or not. Certainly it had been painful. But he'd had no other choice. He'd realized over Thanksgiving that as long as he continued to pursue her, she was going to hold back. While still at her parents' house, she had warned him that the future might get in their way. That was when he'd known if he didn't do something drastic, it *would* get in their way again because she would let it.

Well, she'd had three weeks to herself, time enough to think things over. Now they were going to have to resolve the future. He would stop by to see her tomorrow on his way back from the airport.

Adrienne glanced up when the doorbell sounded, then down at her shapeless navy sweat shirt and jogging pants. Her hair was still damp from her shower. Not that it made a great deal of difference what she looked like, she decided as she pushed herself wearily out of the chair. It was probably only Kelly.

It wasn't. Christopher stood at the door, looking polished and urbane in a camel wool coat and plaid cashmere scarf.

"Hello. I hope I'm not interrupting anything," he said.

For a moment her eyes clung to his face, devouring all the little details: the high bridge of his nose; the way his dark hair curled over his collar; the length of his eyelashes. Although her hand remained slack at her side, it itched to reach out and trace the perfect curve of his jaw.

One dark eyebrow arched questioningly. *"Am* I interrupting something?"

"No, I don't think so," she said numbly. That was an idiotic answer, of course, she told herself. She would *know* if he were interrupting something.

"Good." He stepped inside. "It's still snowing out," he reported pleasantly.

"Is it?" *I'm turning into a brilliant conversationalist,* Adrienne reflected wryly. But what did he expect? She should be angry with him for ignoring her for three weeks, then showing up on her doorstep looking so damnably cheerful. But she was too relieved to be anything but glad to see him.

"I hope you don't mind my dropping in unexpectedly," he said as he pulled off his gloves. "May I put my suitcase in your bathroom? It's pretty wet, so I hate to set it on the hardwood floor."

"Suitcase?" For the first time she noticed the handsome leather suitcase. Something caught in her throat. "Are—are you going somewhere?"

"Just got back."

She breathed a deep sigh of relief. So *that* was why he hadn't called her. But his next words dispelled that hope.

"I flew out yesterday and got in today." He disappeared into the bathroom with the suitcase and returned a moment later. "Quite a snarl at O'Hare. Say, you wouldn't happen to have something hot to drink, would you?"

"Uh, yes, I'll fix some hot chocolate." But she remained rooted to the living room floor. Now that she was over the shock of seeing him, she wanted to understand what was going on. "Then you've only been out of town overnight?"

"Uh-huh." He pulled off his muted plaid scarf and began unbuttoning his coat.

Although she already knew the answer, she forced herself to frame the question. "Otherwise you've been in town since Thanksgiving?"

"Yes, why?"

Adrienne made a feeble attempt to shrug. "No reason." Immediately her shifting, uncertain emotions began to congeal into irritation at herself. Why was she lying to him? There was a reason, and why was she hiding it? "Well, I am a little curious why you haven't called me." That ought to win an award as the world's greatest understatement, she thought with a derisive smile. She'd been miserable for the past three weeks, and here he came gliding into her house as if nothing were wrong. Damn him. And damn her, too, for letting him.

There was dead silence in the room as Christopher laid his coat on the sofa, then turned back to her. "I guess I didn't know what to say to you," he began quietly. "You see, I've been offered a job in Chicago. I went up there for an interview."

"Are—are you going . . . to take the job?" Her voice broke in mid-sentence. The heartache of the last three weeks paled to insignificance beside the thought of losing Christopher forever. As long as he remained in St. Louis, surely they could work something out.

"I don't know."

Adrienne wrung her hands together helplessly. She didn't understand any of this. "But—you can't!"

One eyebrow lifted in question. "Why not?"

"Because—you just can't." For an instant she thought she saw disappointment register in his eyes, as if he had been hoping for another answer. What did he want her to say—that she loved him? She did, but she was afraid to tell him that. She wanted him to say the words first, before she laid her true feelings on the line.

"You've never been happy with the fact that you and I are in competition here," he pointed out calmly. My taking the job in Chicago might be the ideal solution for us."

Adrienne felt a wave of helpless fury. She wanted to shout at him and throw things, but she did neither. Instead, she stood rigidly, her words barely audible. "This is what comes of loving people. They always hurt you." This was what she had feared all along; she had followed her feelings, and now she was being punished.

He started to move toward her, then checked himself. "Not always, Adrienne."

She tasted something warm and salty and realized that she was crying. What was the use? she asked herself as she wiped the tears from her cheeks. "But you're le-leaving," she said brokenly. It was hard to keep him in focus because of the mist in her eyes, but she thought he looked as bleak and unhappy as she felt. Why was he making them both miserable?

"I won't go if you ask me to stay, Adrienne."

She looked at him questioningly, too cautious to believe the answer was so simple. "You know I want you to stay," she whispered.

He took a deep breath. "Then I'll stay, but there's a condition. I'll stay only if you love me—love me enough to commit yourself to me forever." In a single step he covered the distance between them and wrapped her in his arms. His tone softened to a caress. "Forget the condition," he said hoarsely. "Just don't cry. I can't bear it when you're so unhappy. I'll stay if you just tell me you like me a little bit. Honey, please don't cry," he mumbled plaintively.

She couldn't help it. The tears were a release from the past three weeks of anxiety, soul-searching, and loneliness. Although his arms were strong and comforting around her, she could hear the pain in his pleas and knew that he hurt as much as she did.

"Darling, hush. It's all right." He folded her closer against him. "I didn't mean to hurt you. Believe me, I wouldn't hurt you for the world. I love you too much for that."

She brushed her wet cheek against his shoulder and tried to absorb it all. He loved her, and he wanted her, and she wasn't going to lose him. The words were fragments of knowledge that had to be assimilated slowly before she could understand them on an emotional level. He actually loved her! And she wasn't going to lose him to Chicago or anyone else—not if she told him she loved him, too.

He cupped his hand around the back of her head. "Adrienne, say something, please."

She took a wavering breath and blinked back new tears. "I do love you, Christopher. More than I've ever loved anyone, but I thought—" She dissolved into tears again. Only now they were tears of relief, and they cleansed her of pain she had been holding back for far longer than three weeks.

"Adrienne, don't!" he begged in a stricken voice. "It tears me up to hear you cry like that."

"I'm s-s-sorry."

He led her to the sofa with a gentle hand on the small of her back. And then, because he couldn't think of anything else to do, he let her cry.

It was five full minutes before Adrienne turned a tear-soaked face up to his. He had told her he loved her, and she had confessed her love for him. At last the radiance of those words began to dawn in her eyes, bringing a slow, rapturous smile to her lips.

When he smiled back at her, he looked achingly handsome. "You are going to marry me, aren't you?" he asked as he twisted one of her curls around his finger.

She blinked dewy lashes. "Oh, yes!"

"Good." He sighed and enveloped her in a fierce hug.

As if she would try to get away, she thought with a blissful smile. A moment later, however, her smile faded. "But why didn't you just ask me three weeks ago instead of making me suffer like this?"

He put her away from him and studied her searchingly. "Would you have said yes then?"

"Of course—" Pausing, she thought back to what she had told him in her parents' backyard: that she couldn't be sure about the future. Maybe she wouldn't have said yes. Even as recently as Thanksgiving she had been hedging her emotions. She hadn't really admitted to herself that she loved him until just now. "I don't know," she confessed honestly.

"I didn't either, and I couldn't afford to take the chance."

She smoothed back the rich black hair from his temple. "So what about Chicago?" she asked with a faint smile.

"Do you want to live there?"

Her finger trailed on down to the sensual curve of his masculine jaw. "Not particularly, but if that's where you're going, then I'm darn sure going there, too."

His smile deepened immeasurably. "What if I stay at KTOO?" he asked.

She tried pursing her lips to hold back her smile. "Then I'll just have to keep you in your place in the ratings."

"There's another possibility," he confided as he slipped his hand beneath her chin, then took a moment to steal a lingering kiss. "I've been offered a job at a local television station—Channel Fifty-nine."

Her eyes widened. "Fifty-nine! But that's the lowest-ranking station in town! I've heard it's about to go under. Besides, you don't know anything about television and—" She clamped her mouth shut on a giggle. Of course, Channel 59 was the lowest-ranking station in town. She wouldn't have expected Christopher to take on anything less than a challenge. And so what if he didn't

190

know anything about television? She had every confidence he would learn.

As if he had followed her logic step by step, he said, "Good, then it's settled. Want to kiss the groom?"

"Well, maybe just one chaste kiss," she conceded and daintily pressed her lips to his.

He took over from there, displaying a wealth of desire that mirrored her own pent-up passion.

"You know," she whispered when his lips feathered away from hers to dally at her ear. "I think I like being in love with you."

"I intend to make sure that you do."